Jaime Adoff

JUMP AT THE SUN
HYPERION PAPERBACKS

New York

Library of Congress Cataloging-in-Publication Data on file.
This book is set in Sabon.
Designed by Ellice M. Lee
First Hyperion Paperbacks edition, 2007
1 3 5 7 9 10 8 6 4 2
Printed in the United States of America
ISBN-13: 978-1-4231-0400-1
ISBN-10: 1-4231-0400-5

Visit www.hyperionteens.com

FOR MARI

CHAPTER

boxes

Everywhere I look, I trip over them,

and land on more.

Our life now—nothing but boxes.

Everything we own, everything we can grab—

miles of tape close up our past.

Mom cries as Aunt Berny puts her arm around her.

Mom pulls away, cutting another piece of tape.

I watch it all happen, like a silent news reporter.

Taking everything in, not able to really deal.

Not able to deal with it at all.

I'm alone now. Lost without Dad.

All alone, just me inside my head.

Mom says everything is going to be different now.

Mom says everything has changed.

Mom says a lot more with her eyes than her mouth.

Her eyes so sad all the time.

Looking down, looking anywhere but here.

NOW,

this time that came so fast,

snuck up on us and took away my Dad.

Took away our life.

I hate here

I hate now

I hate all these

boxes.

whisper house

Our house used to be all loud and everything.

Music blasting, singing—laughing.

Now we have the Whisper House.

Just whispers everywhere.

Mom thinks I can't hear what she's saying,

but I can.

Like how the bank is going to take our house,

and

what happened to all the money we had?

Our life savings gone in a flash.

And

how are we going to make it?

Whispers drift in on pain and worry.

Mom thinks it's gonna be real hard on me.

Thirteen, growin' up without a dad.

The whispers are so loud.

Louder than the music used to be.

That's hard to believe;

but it's true.

the music

that was everything. This house *was* music.

Dad downstairs, in the studio.

Dad lookin' for the next big thing.

The new hot band.

A hit, so he could retire.

Always talkin' about retiring.

But Dad did well.

He liked to teach me about the music biz.

"Just a little school for ya," he'd say.

Made his money with his music publishing deals.

Royalties from songs on the radio.

I thought ASCAP was the name of Dad's best friend,

the way he would tear open the envelopes

to get his checks.

Dad had bands that he got signed to record deals.

He got paid from that, too.

Dad did alright for himself
and for us.
I always had the best stuff, the hottest games
and coolest toys.
Dad was in his heyday when I was younger.
He was *rollin' in the dough*—I can still see him
droppin' to the floor, rollin' around the carpet.
Laughin' like he just said something *so* funny.
Then he'd get up quick and
deliver one of his famous lines:
"You never know in this business;
one day you're hot,
one day you're not.
So enjoy it while I got!"
Mom said he'd be a music producer till the day he
died.
Mom was right.

Boomin' and thumpin' bass
sneakin' through the soundproof walls.
Just enough to make your head start movin'
while you were watchin' TV.

The sound track to my everyday.

Pretty cool compared to what most dads do.

I can still hear that bass sometimes.

When it's quiet.

Like now. I can feel it in my chest.

In my ears—straining to hear the music

from the studio. As quiet as Dad is now.

Still

like Brooklawn cemetery.

Dad's final resting place.

have you ever been
(to electric ladyland)

I have.

Dad took me once.

Electric Lady Studios, downtown on Eighth Street.

Used to be a club, then Jimi came along,

waved his magic wand

and turned it into one of the greatest studios ever.

Jimi

Hendrix.

The greatest guitarist

who ever lived.

Dad's favorite artist of all time.

I could listen to Jimi all day and night.

Jimi and me are a lot alike:

left-handers who love to write

poetry and music.

Both of us falling in love at a very young age.

Falling in love with our

six-string girls.

Jimi was part Cherokee.

Dad said he was, too.

I can hear Dad tellin' me to get close;

"Check out my high cheekbones."

Dad's voice in my head

sounding so

clear

so

close

so

real.

Dad and Jimi were like brothers

who never knew each other.

Black hippies with big souls and even bigger smiles.
Peace and love and all that other stuff
nobody talks about anymore.
Both died
way before their time.
Jimi at twenty-seven.
Dad made it to forty-nine.
Still, way too young to die.

Jimi did it to himself.
Or so they say.
(I think it was just a tragic mistake.)
Dad never saw it comin'.
Guess in the end it doesn't matter, does it?
Dead is dead.
And Jimi said:

> *The magic carpet waits for you*
> *so don't you be late*

Is that what you ride when you die?
I know Jimi was talkin' about love;
but
I'm talkin' about death—on my mind

all the time, now.

Maybe Dad and Jimi are up in Heaven,

havin' a big-ass jam session.

Or

maybe

Dad's just dead.

Cold and dark.

No

sound

no

air

no

nothin'.

reality sucks

that's probably why we dream.

Why our bodies need sleep.

So we can escape.

Escape this earth, at least for a little while.

Every night, we get to go away.

Sleep is the only time I feel safe.

The only time I can leave this place.

This reality that feels like needles

sticking into my flesh.

This hell that is so hot it makes my hair sweat.

Makes my mind melt.

In my sleep I hear music, I see faces,

songs and

smiles

and

Dad hugging me tight.

Never letting me go.

Telling me to be strong.

Telling me not to give up

hope.

Sometimes I wake up crying.

Sometimes I wish I didn't wake up

at all.

it comes in waves

like the ocean.

No.

More like electricity.

Shocking me,

making me want to

hurt myself or someone else—

We interrupt this regularly scheduled program

to bring you

Keith James, destroying everything in his path . . .

dubbed the hurricane of death. . . .

James is described as a seemingly shy kid who,

by all accounts, just snapped.

More on this story at eleven. . . .

See, that's what I'm talking about. That was a wave.

More like a tidal wave.

Always hits when I least expect it.

Thinking about death and revenge.

Making someone else feel my pain, my hurt

makes me feel

better

worse

makes me feel

something.

More on this story as it develops. . . .

dad's words

"You have to channel your energy . . .

Turn a negative into a positive."

Dad's voice in my head

all the time now.

Freaks me out

but I like it, too.

"Channel your energy/your pain/your hurt.

Violence never solved a thing. Just listen to what

Jimi sings. . . ."

Violence never solved a thing.

Maybe not,

but it might feel good.

Who am I kidding?

Don't have the stones to really do something.

Not like in Rolling

but

balls/*cajones.*

I'm not a lover or a fighter.

I'm just a singer in a rock 'n' roll band.

Well, not exactly. I try to be a singer.

Guitar player, too. But no band.

Need to talk to people, make friends to start a band.

"Life isn't a spectator sport. . . ."

Dad talkin' again.

Givin' out wisdom from beyond the grave.

See what happens when you get in the game?

You get yourself shot.

Shot dead.

That's what happens.

Sorry, Dad, I didn't mean that.

sometimes it hits me

It was my fault.

I killed my dad.

It hits me hard

and takes so long

to go away.

Hours trying to justify

that I had nothing to do with it.

Hours trying to understand how I could have let this
happen to him.

I couldn't even save my own dad.

I didn't do a damn thing.

I should have woken up;

Mom should have woke me up,

told me Dad was going out.

I shouldn't have gone to bed that night.

I should have just stayed up.

Should have just stayed up until everyone was safe;

until I knew for sure

Dad was

okay.

I should have stopped him,

I could have stopped him.

Guilt

stops *me* cold.

Hits me hard.

It was my fault.

I killed my dad.

CHAPTER 2

from pause to play

It's like everything was off, and now it's back on.

From pause to play

the days starting again.

My life a DVD, forcing me to watch.

Making me a part

of this Nightmare on James Street.

I'm one of the main characters.

One of the few that's left.

That isn't dead.

I wonder what's gonna happen next.

I know we are moving.

In two days my life will change.

But what's gonna happen after that?

Who's gonna get it next?

I wish I could just fast-forward

to the end.

nasty food and kind words

Strangers coming in and out.

Suits and ties pretend to be friends.

They say they're here to help,

but they just make my mom cry—more.

Half the time they call me by the wrong name.

I wish they'd leave us alone.

Mom's friends try to help—bringing food

and kind words.

Nasty food I don't want to eat.

Mom doesn't like it either, I think.

But she says thanks.

We both do.

Mom's best friend, Dorothy, can't even set foot

in the house—

"Too many memories," she says.

Sometimes I hear Mom whispering on the phone,

talking to Dorothy.

Talking about what's going to happen to us.

Talking about Dad.

Mom tries to act like she hasn't been crying,

but I can see her eyes, all red and puffy.

Mom tries to act like everything's normal,

talking about the weather. . . .

Mom

tries.

cool all over

Aunt Berny is talkin' a mile a minute—loud, too.

She's kinda crazy, but she's cool.

Dad's only sister. She's like Mom's sister, too.

Aunt Berny is always positive, talkin' like

everything's gonna be okay.

Nothing will ever be okay again.

"Little Cool, you are gonna' love Hollow Falls."

Aunt Berny always calls me Little Cool.

Dad called me that, too.

Dad used to say, "'Cause you little, and you cool."

That's me, Little Cool—five foot two

(on a good day),

caramel brown Frap-pu-ccino face—**BIG, bushy** 'fro

gone wild, and it's never comin' back.

Aunt Berny says I'm the best of both worlds:

black and white and coooool all over.

day after tomorrow

That's when we move to Hollow Falls, Ohio.

Sounds like some horror-movie town to me.

Where everyone gets sliced up at night.

Livin' in log cabins by some creepy-ass lake.

Nobody asked me if *I* wanted to move.

What's wrong with Brooklyn, anyway?

This is my home.

This brownstone is home.

Aunt Berny and Mom are tryin' to sugarcoat it.

Tryin' to make it sound like such a nice place to live.

So quiet.

So safe.

I feel myself getting hot—

not from these August dog days;

hot

from the inside out.

I'm about to explode;

but I try to stuff it back down.

Stuff it back inside.

Back to where it can't hurt anyone.

But

me.

"*i'm not goin'*"

The words come fast and mean.

Like a storm from the clear blue sky. . . .
Now I am running towards my room.
I want to punch something
but there's nothin' to punch.
Everything all packed away.
Aunt Berny starts after me—
"Just let him be."
Mom's words follow me
upstairs, but *she* doesn't.
I slam the door and dive into bed.
Wrap my head in my pillow and bury myself
under
the covers.
My eyes sting as I flip to the dry side.
Dad should be recording tonight.
He used to let me listen in on his sessions
sometimes.
Dad shouldn't have taken a break.
He should have stayed inside.
He should have stayed inside with me and Mom.
He should be here now.
He can't be gone.

He can't be

gone. . . .

aunt berny knocks
but I don't answer.
I don't want to talk to anyone.
Even Aunt Berny.
She knocks again.
Opening the door slowly, like she's checking for
booby traps.
I don't wanna talk;
nothin' to say.
I feel the bed sink down. Covers pulling to one side.
Aunt Berny speaks slow and quiet:
"Everything's gonna be okay, Cool.
You know I lost him, too.
I feel the same as you."
Aunt Berny has this way. She always did.
Ever since I could remember.
This way about her. Like a slow waterfall.
Just calms you right down.

I sit up and Aunt Berny puts her arm around me.
She smells like onions. Must be cookin' supper.
Aunt Berny holds me tight and tells me it'll be okay.
I wish it would be okay.
But I know it won't.
It'll never be okay again.

like a middle linebacker
The bed sounds like it's cracking,
buckling from the weight.
Aunt Berny's not light.
She's not fat; just solid.
Short and stocky, kinda like a middle linebacker.
Aunt Berny's a trip;
wearin' those tight-fitting shirts.
Almost see-through too.
Her and Uncle Carl split,
so she's tryin' to be hip again.
She looks like a big grape, if you ask me;
but I would never say that to her face.
I'm short, but I'm not stupid.

now is not the time

I want to ask Aunt Berny what happened with her
and Uncle Carl,
and what Hollow Falls is really like.
Dad said it was a serious redneck place.
I want to ask Aunt Berny what it's like for
black folks there.
What it's like for biracial folks, like me.
I want to ask her a lot of things,
but not now.
Now Aunt Berny is holding Mom's hand.
And they're both crying.
Quiet crying in front of the TV.
The news is talkin' about all the bad stuff
the news always talks about.
Almost eleven-thirty.
So many things I want to ask.
But now is not the time.

the night before the night before

I close my eyes tight and see Dad.
Like he was.

Not how he is—now.

Six foot two with a goofy smile.

(I take after Grandma May—too-SHORT)

Dad was always workin' on a song.

Didn't have to be in the studio, either.

On the phone, tappin' his foot

to some beat in his head,

some beat only he could hear.

At dinner: his knife and fork were two drumsticks,

Dad bobbin' his head as he chewed.

Dad always had a tune to sing.

"Hey Cool, check this out," he'd say to me.

Dad could sound like any instrument.

FOOMP UMP SKAT

FOOMP FOOMP UMP SKAT

CHICKA

FOOMP UMP SKAT

FOOMP FOOMP UMP SKAT.

Layin' down the beat first.

Then playin' his imaginary bass

BOOM BOOMP

BAAAAAAAAAAAAHH

OOOM BOOMP.

Some wicked-funky bass line.
Never played the same thing twice.
Dad could sing, too.
Had this high falsetto thing he'd do.
Smooth like the smoothest R&B.
Never saw him write a thing
down.
Had it all in his head.
He just had it like that.
I close my eyes the night before the night before
the move.
Dad is testin' out his latest tune.
I bob my head
and groove myself to sleep. . . .

dad's alive
Dad's still here.
I know he's still here.
Close by.
Probably down in the studio.

Have to ask him about my demo.

We're almost done.

Just have to add a couple more tracks.

Can't wait to see him.

Seems like a long time.

Too long.

I smell bacon.

Mom's cookin' breakfast.

Bacon and eggs.

Me and Dad's favorite.

Can't wait to see him.

Feels like a long time since I've seen him.

How come it feels like it's been so long?

good morning

Aunt Berny is smiling down at me.

I'm not expecting a face looking at me

when I open my eyes.

Her smiling face makes me sit bolt upright.

My heart starts beating fast.

What is she doing here?

I didn't know she was visiting.

Slowly it comes back.

The seconds stretching over days

and weeks.

Almost a month now . . .

The good feeling

turns bad.

Real bad.

That sick feeling in the pit of my stomach.

Not even the smell of bacon and eggs

can take that away.

The bad is all around me now.

Choking me.

Squeezing my neck.

Tightening my chest.

Aunt Berny's face changes.

"Little Cool—breathe." Aunt Berny screams.

I wake up like this sometimes.

Like now.

Can't catch

my

breath.

Snot and tears soak up my pillow

as Mom runs into my room.

She puts a paper bag over my nose and mouth.

"Breathe slowly, baby, just take your time."

I feel the noose loosen around my neck.

Starting to get my air again.

Sitting up, they both rub and pat my back.

Like I was a little kid.

But I'm the man of the house.

Last one standing

at least for now. . . .

I crumple up the bag,

fly down the stairs,

and run outside.

Breathing in the fresh, polluted New York air.

I suck it in through my lips.

I must look crazy in my pajamas,

standin' out on the sidewalk.

But I need some air.

Only got a day left to breathe in the good stuff.

I scared myself just then.

Thought I was gonna die.

Always think I'm gonna die these days.

Things happen so fast.

You never know.

One day you're here.

One day

you're not.

One day you're singin'.

One day

you're shot. . . .

Sounds like a hit record to me.

Snot drips down from my nose

takes the back entrance

into my throat.

I spit on the street and make my way back inside.

Mom looks worried

Aunt Berny does, too.

I walk past both of them, up the stairs to my room.

Under the covers.

Trying to fall back asleep.

Then I can wake up again

and forget.

At least

for a few seconds.

dead man walking

The day goes slow.

This day before.

Slow like math class.

Painfully slow.

Everyone knows what tomorrow is.

Everyone knows I don't wanna go.

But I don't get to vote.

Our house is busy.

But not the good kind.

Busy like

on death row, the day before

an execution.

That kind of busy.

Doin' what needs to get done.

Even though it's hard to do,

you do it.

Packin' and makin' sure nothin' gets left behind.

I wish they'd leave me behind.

How can I move to Ohio when Dad is

here?

How am I gonna visit his grave?

How is he gonna know where I am?
Two o'clock and I'm out of appeals.

Wonder if I get to choose *my*
last meal.

where's mom?
Seems like she's gone AWOL since Dad was killed.
Just out of reach.
Out of touch
with me.
Maybe Mom can't handle being a mom anymore.
Maybe that's what happens when your husband gets
taken from you
so fast,
so young.
So,
where's Mom?
I'm still her son.
There's still someone left.
There's still
me.

my guitar

Sitting silent for the first time.

The last thing I need to pack.

I should just put it in its case.

I can't play,

not now, anyway.

Every time I look at my electric,

it reminds me of Dad.

My screamin' red flyin' V—

the one Dad got me for my ninth birthday.

(I should have asked for a Les Paul, but what did I

know, I was only nine.)

Autographed by Anthony Sartinelli—fastest hands

in the world.

"The fretboard fiend,"

according to *Guitar Gods* magazine.

I guess now I've got a lot of guitars, all of Dad's.

The ones in the studio and—

I feel tears wanting to come out for an encore,

but I push them back.

The smell of some serious Aunt Berny throw-down

sneaks underneath my door

and into my nose.
I don't know if I can eat,
but I'll try.
Need my strength.
Need to be strong;
Gotta be strong.

dinner

We sit and eat, and try not to think too much about
the future
or the past,
or anything.
Mom tries to eat, but gives up after a few bites.
With her hair pulled back
her face looks long and sad.
Her gray getting grayer by the day
her face looks gray, too.
Like ash from a fire that never washed off.
Talking into the air
Mom says she sent the life insurance claim in.
"Shouldn't be too long," Mom says, pushing her
peas around her plate.

Aunt Berny is cracking jokes, cackling away.

Trying to change the subject,

but

Mom barely smiles.

time passing by

"Movin' day's tomorrow," Aunt Berny says

between spoonfuls of mac and cheese.

"Things are gonna get hectic,

but before you know it, you'll be in

Hollow Falls, Ohio,

and you both are gonna have a real fine life there.

Don't you worry, things are gonna be real fine."

Real fine. Yeah, right.

How am I gonna have a real fine life there?

How could I ever have a real fine life—without Dad.

What about my friends?

Okay, there's only two of them, but—

What about my band?

Okay, I didn't have one yet, but—

Dad was gonna help me, he was gonna—

I swallow my mac and cheese, and bite my tongue.

Wouldn't matter anyway. Doesn't matter what *I* say.
Won't change a thing.
I look at Mom, and she looks tired and small.
Skin and
bones starting to show through.
Her pants hanging on for dear life—
her face sunken in.
Aunt Berny is smiling at me,
her smile is warm like a big fuzzy blanket.
Something you can crawl under,
wrap yourself up in—her smile,
trying to make things alright, trying hard
to make things seem better than they are.
Her smile
helps.
Nobody says a word. Seems like forever,
we just sit, and stare,
listening to the kitchen clock tick away the seconds,
and minutes
and
time passing by, so fast.

I wish tomorrow didn't have to come so soon.

I wish tomorrow didn't have to come at all.

CHAPTER **3**

midnight snack

Me and Mom, looking for a midnight snack.

I couldn't sleep.

Just lying in bed, hoping the morning never comes.

I pour the cereal into a bowl—one for Mom,

one for me.

Moving one month to the day. The twenty-first.

That's a cruel joke, but right now

I *have* to know.

the question

"What happened?"

I ask, listening to my cereal snap and crackle and—

Mom knows exactly what I'm asking.

Mom knows . . .

The **question** floats above our heads,

hanging on to pain and hurt,

blood and tears.

The **answer** waiting for its chance—to inflict more

damage.

Waiting like the devil himself.

The devil's in the details—

like Aunt Berny always says.

Details I don't want to—but have to—

know.

My cereal bowl is almost empty,

as the question slides

down the kitchen walls,

landing like a brick in Mom's lap.

Mom shifts in her seat, looking uncomfortable.

Almost in pain.

Like the answer is wrapped so tightly

around her neck.

It's starting to choke her.

She opens the fridge

and pretends to be looking for something.

Maybe she's looking for the answer—

right behind the milk,

or next to the eggs.

She shuts the fridge and scoots her chair closer to

mine.

Her nose just inches from my face.

Inches away . . .

stalling

Mom is stalling, I can tell.

Wanting to *wait* to talk about this until we get to

Ohio.

Mom wants me to see a shrink too.

I'm not crazy, I don't need to see a stupid shrink.

"What was Dad doin' over by the Corner?

He knows not to go there.

He's the one who always said not to go over there

after dark.

Ever since I was a little kid he said,

'Never go to the left. Never go to the left.'

What was he doin' there?"

My words come out rapid-fire.

Almost coming out faster than I can say them.

Coming way too fast for Mom.

She moves back, a few inches.

Like maybe she was too close for comfort.

Her comfort.

Mom looks confused.

Like she doesn't know where to begin.

Like she doesn't *want* to begin.

Squeezing her face tight—she shuts her eyes.

I know she wishes I would just disappear.

A magic trick to get her off the hook.

Then she wouldn't have to begin

or

end.

The kitchen clock sounds louder all of a sudden.

The minute hand moves again.

More silence from her end.

See, she's just stalling,

I can tell.

killer's corner

Her voice is weak,

her words come slow and jumbled.

But I hear what she's saying.

What she's trying to tell me.

Nino's was out of Diet Coke.

Dad went over by the Corner

another deli.

Dad always jonesin' for his Diet Coke. . . .

"Some thugs up to no good.

I told him it wasn't safe. I told him . . .

They just had a shooting over there

two nights before, too. . . .

He knew—I told him.

He promised he wouldn't go over there anymore.

Told him I'd buy him a case of Diet Coke. . . .

Just went from bad to worse.

Bad to worse.

Your father was in the wrong place

at the wrong time.

That's it.

Just the wrong place at the wrong time. . . .

Just a stupid Diet Coke— He always felt so safe here.

Like nothin' bad could ever happen—

like Brooklyn was someplace in Canada,

for God's sake.

I told him it wasn't safe.

Why didn't he listen to me?

Why did he think they called it Killer's Corner?

People get killed there.

Why didn't you listen to me?

Why?"

Mom is looking right at me,
talkin' like she's talkin' to Dad
and
it's freaking me out.
Her face is full of pain,
she's squinting her eyes,
closing them even tighter now.
Part of me wants to just let it go.
But
I have to know.

the answer
I don't want to hear her words
attacking my ears
attacking me.
The truth hurts.
It really does . . .
"Those thugs just came in to rob the place.
But the store owner wouldn't open the register;
that's when things got bad.
Your father, he was first in line,
just put his money down on the counter when . . ."

I'm only hearing bits and pieces.

But it's already too much.

I want to run out of the kitchen,

run out of the house;

get as far away from here as I can.

But I don't move.

I just sit.

Still and quiet.

Listening to Mom.

"That's when the shooting started.

Bullets flying everywhere . . . Took most of them

in the chest—

He was the closest . . . he was too close . . .

Fell down, right where he stood.

Right where he stood."

bullets in my sleep

When I close my eyes

I see bullets and death and

Dad's chest ripping apart.

I see Mom's tears and pain

and I can't make it go away.

I wish I never would have asked that question.

POP

I wake up mad.

One month today.

One-month anniversary.

Only one month, and now we have to move.

I miss him and

hate him at the same time.

Maybe not really hate.

But,

yeah, sometimes I think it is.

A kind of hate.

Get so mad at Dad for

gettin' himself shot up.

And for what?

A soda, that's what.

It hurts so much.

Hurts in this place I never felt before.

Some place deep I didn't know was there.

Dad went to the Corner to buy a soda pop
Dad went to the Corner and got himself shot.

Could be a street nursery rhyme.
Let this be a lesson to you kiddies.
Soda pop can kill.
pop-pop/pop/pop/pop/
pop-pop/pop/pop/

p

o

p

.

good-bye
I'm up early, before Mom and the sun.
Before the movers come and take away our life,
put it in a truck and drive it away
to some place I've never been before.
Someplace I don't even want to go to.
Someplace, else.

I am stumbling from room to room—looking
for something, I don't know what.
Wide awake saying good-bye to this place.

dad's footsteps
Sometimes my eyes play tricks on me.
My ears do, too. Like now.
I hear footsteps.
Dad's footsteps coming up from the basement.
Clunking up those stairs.
Up from the basement.
Up from his "office." The studio.
State of the art everything—the highest of high tech.
Dad's footsteps getting louder.
I can almost see his face.
I can almost see him
as he passes me on his way to the kitchen.
My demo almost done/layin' down tracks
right before that night.
That night that never ends.
Playing over and over again—
the police on the phone;

Mom screaming and crying and—

I hear footsteps, this time they're mine.

Walking down to the basement.

Looking for Dad.

Even though I know

he's not there.

studio for sale

Mom is selling everything.

Dad's pride and joy,

going piece by piece.

A room full of holes where equipment used to be.

Big empty spaces and silence.

I wish Mom didn't have to sell off the studio.

Everything Dad put into it, that was his life.

Mom says *we* won't have a life if she doesn't sell it.

"We've got no choice."

Mom's words way too real for my ears. . . .

Dad's swivel chair is still here.

I sit and swivel like he used to do.

Scratch my head like Dad.

Thinking about making "the next big hit."

Dad's big hit always "just around the bend."
In the basement, I'm wandering, looking,
hoping to find anything—nothing,
something, maybe of Dad's.
Something that maybe he wanted me to have.
I feel like I'm back in the past
still waiting for Dad to come

just around the bend. . . .

the trunk

I see it in the corner, tons of junk on top.
Dust so thick it makes me sneeze.
I know what it is as soon as I see it.
Haven't seen it for a *long* time.
I remember from years back,
when Dad would pull stuff out of it.
Like a magic show.
Dad's trunk full of magic and surprises and
Hendrix.
I can almost stick my whole head inside.
The trunk is huge.

Big fluffy hats with feathers, and scarves,

tie-dyed shirts, and leather pants.

Dad's treasure chest.

Jimi Hendrix posters and patches.

Old records, CDs, and tapes.

All kinds of great stuff.

My mind goes back

to

me and Dad and

Jimi *was baaaaaaaaad* . . .

i flashback

to a long time gone.

Dad jumps off the sofa, playin' his guitar

crashes down

onto the soft carpet floor.

Me and Mom holler and laugh and can barely stand

up

we can barely stand.

Jammin' to the '60s jams.

Dad's favorite bands.

Singin' along with

Joplin and Dylan.

Sly

and the Family Stone.

Dad pickin' his teeth

with guitar strings—singin' to his hero,

the greatest of them all . . .

JIMI

HENDRIX

The first black rock star.

Dad knew all his tunes,

looked like him, too.

Crazy/wild/so much style—just like

Jimi.

I flash-forward to this second:

starin' hard at Dad and Jimi,

that picture used to hang on the studio wall.

Now it's on the floor.

That picture taken at the wax museum

some vacation

I can't even remember now. . . .

I stare hard,

then I have to look away.

hendrix

was like one of the family.

Dad talked about him like he was.

"His music meant so much," Dad would say.

Bridged the gap

brought people together . . .

A true genius . . .

He took the guitar and rode it to the moon . . .

Changed the face of rock 'n' roll.

No one has ever come close

to Jimi.

Not just another dead rock star.

He still shines bright.

His power

pulling me deeper into the trunk.

Deeper into the past.

Closer to

Jimi,

closer

to Dad.

music sweet music

I crank up my DigiTunes.

1,000 songs to go.

Dad's last present to me.

"Fully loaded with the best of the best," Dad said.

I click the "Hendrix" playlist

and crank it UP.

Playing my air guitar,

listenin' to Jimi sing;

> Music sweet music, I wish I could caress . . .
>
> caress, caress . . .

If I had my guitar I think I might play, for real.

My guitar's packed away, finally—

ready for the move.

They're goin' with Aunt Berny.

She's gonna take Dad's guitars, too.

I hear Aunt Berny and Mom getting up,

doors shutting, water running—showers on.

I grab what I can of Jimi and Dad,

close the trunk then run up the stairs, two at a time.

movin's not on my mind

just

    music sweet

    music sweet

    music . . .

    sweet

    music . . .

CHAPTER 4

MAJ

"You better be careful, sometimes there's cops on
I-80."

Mom looks nervous, her voice cracking with every
other word.

Mom looks unsure about Vic, the moving guy.

Aunt Berny hookin' us up with an old friend.

Hookin' us up with a serious discount.

Mom says we need discounts now.

"I'll slow down for ya. Don't worry,

I can still get us there in time.

I'm real sorry to hear about your husband. . . .

I didn't know Marvin that well."

Marvin. Almost didn't know who that was.

That's Dad. But nobody called him Marvin.

Everyone called him MAJ.

Short for Marvin Anthony James

Dad said it was short for

MAJ-ic.

Dad was magic in the studio.

He used to say he could make a skunk smell sweet,

and *sound* even better.

Times were getting tough, but he was still
one of the best.
Everybody knew that.
MAJ the magic man,
my dad.

don't even need to close my eyes
to see my dad.
Listenin' to Jimi sing "Highway Chile":
    His guitar slung across his back
    His dusty boots is his Cadillac
    . . . He's a highway chile
    . . . Highway chile
    . . . Walk on brother
Starin' straight out the window at this long,
boring road.
I see Dad drivin' in a Jeep passing right by me.
Wavin' as he goes.
Dad liked to wave.
He'd give you one of those just-a-minute waves
when he was busy.

Which was most of the time.

Dad was always busy.

With music/recording/rehearsing/or

trying to book an artist to record.

Dad was always at the club, too.

Out checkin' for fresh talent.

Sometimes he'd roll in at four in the morning

on the weekends.

Part of the gig. So weird I can hear his voice.

Like he's talkin' to me.

But only I can hear him.

We should have had more time.

Time for some of the fun stuff.

Dad always said we'd do more fun stuff as soon as

the next project was done.

But there was always a next project.

And a next project after that.

He took me to see the Yankees, once. But they lost.

Dad was on his cell the whole time.

Part of the gig . . . I guess,

part of the gig. . . .

invisible knives

Mom just starting to relax,

as Vic guns it past a slow-moving car.

She grabs my arm, the G-force sucks us back

into the cramped front seat.

Me and Mom like two astronauts

blasting off, down Interstate-80,

on our way to Hollow Falls, Ohio.

Going so fast I bet the cars we pass

can't read the CHARIOT'S ON TIRES,

printed on the side of the truck.

This thing's got some giddyup, that's for sure.

Vic's got a half-eaten tuna-fish sandwich

in one hand,

the other on the steering wheel.

Doin' about eighty-five.

Mom is starin' straight ahead,

just like Vic.

But her stare is different.

She looks like she's still in shock.

Her face frozen, no expression.

Trying so hard, but I can tell.

I can tell her insides are all cut up.

Invisible knives doing their damage.

One cut

at a time.

bumps in the road

Five hours down,

five and a half to go.

We pass a long black car,

reminds me of a limo.

I always wanted to ride in one,

like the rock stars do.

My first limo ride was to bury my dad.

Never thought it would be like that. . . .

Now everything comes flooding back—

that day, the cemetery.

The funeral was

CRAZY.

People screamin' and carryin' on.

Mom was double sad, too.

No one came from her family.

After all these years.

Even dead, they still hate my dad.

How could they hate him?

What did he ever do to them?

Mom says all he did was be black.

I didn't know that was a crime.

I start to taste the salt from my tears.

Drivin' down this road,

I know

something isn't right.

It wasn't supposed to be like this.

Dad always took care of everything.

Made sure everything was straight.

He wouldn't have left us like this.

No money/no house/no life.

I know

something isn't right.

last exit

"You know, it's not forever,

just until we get back on our feet.

Then we'll get our own place, maybe even move

back East."

I nod in between my sniffles.

Mom is quiet.

After a while, she takes my hand,

squeezes my fingers.

Forcing a smile . . .

"He's in heaven now," she says.

I look at her, but I can't speak.

All my words

bottled up

bottled

up

inside of me.

Watching the road pass us by.

Watching the signs.

Last Exit . . .

I think we just rent space.

Just rent space in these bodies.

God is the bank, the ultimate landlord.

When your time is up, he kicks you out.

Kicks you out of your body.

Only your soul gets to make the trip

to the new place.
Dad didn't look nothin' like himself
in that wood box.
Nothin' like *my* dad.
Looked like a balloon with all the air let out of it.
That's what he looked like to me.
I could tell he was far away,
way far away from that body.
Now the tears are comin' down in sheets,
my nose is gettin' all stuffed.
Getting red and looking bigger than it already is.
I gotta' stop all this cryin' mess.
I'm grown, I'm gonna be the man of the house.
I should act like it.
But
I can't stop, tears just keep comin',
like they've got a mind of their own.
Mom holds me close and rubs my arm.
I just keep cryin',
blowin my big nose
all the way down the highway.

flat

Like pancake flat. Maybe even flatter than that.

Flat everywhere, not a hill,

not even a bump on the horizon.

Just flat for as far as the eye can see.

Flat as we make our way south.

Almost to Columbus.

One hour left, and my butt's asleep.

My arm is, too.

Flat and fields of corn, and some kind of beans,

Mom says.

Stupid, if you ask me.

Who cares about corn and beans?

I hate this place already.

"we're here"

Vic's voice and squeaky brakes

float into my dreams.

Me and Dad and Jimi,

jamming at the Garden.

Sold out,

screaming crowd.

Yelling my name . . .

Keith

James . . .

Keith

James . . .

Keith

James—

"Keith, we're here," Mom's voice wakes me up.
Brings me back from Madison Square Garden,
back from Dad.
I forget.
Again.
Maybe
when I open my eyes,
this life will be gone
and the old one will come back.
And
maybe
none of this really happened.

And

maybe

it was all just a horrible nightmare.

"Come on, Keith, let's go."

I sit in the truck for as long as I can.

My eyes still closed.

I try to forget *again*.

Maybe

this time

I won't remember.

aunt berny's place

is small. Two small bedrooms

and a guest room.

If the guest is a miniature baby,

I guess it would be cool.

But if you're me

it sucks.

I want to leave already.

Aunt Berny just moved in.

The split from Uncle Carl's been hard, Mom said;

and now on top of that, her brother's dead.

She's been through a lot.

Never could tell, the way Aunt Berny is.

Always so up/always so happy for the day.

I'm not happy about anything, anymore.

Especially this sorry room.

Upstairs again, but nothin' like home.

It's hot up here too.

Aunt Berny calls to me,

sounding so excited.

So excited I'm here.

I don't want to be mean, she's

all we've got.

I don't want to be mean,

but I don't feel like

being nice.

1st night

and it's already feeling a little weird.

Aunt Berny says that now this is "our" house.

But it's still all of "her" stuff.

We couldn't take a lot of "our" stuff.

Mom sold it all off.

"Just the most necessary things,"

Mom said we could bring.

First night, and I'm not complaining, its just strange.

Trying to fit in to a new place.

Gathering around the dinner table.

Aunt Berny is going on about some town gossip,

Mom is listening hard with both ears.

I'm just layin' back, takin' it all in.

Trying to pretend that everything is going to be

okay, like everybody says.

Trying not to scream *get me out of here*

into my scalloped potatoes.

"This is the start of a new life for all of us."

Aunt Berny raises her glass,

and we all clink them together.

I smile at Mom, and she smiles at me.

I go back for thirds, and I'm not even full yet.

Aunt Berny can cook.

Even better on her home turf.

I'm eating like a machine.

Automatically/without thinking.

It's best not to think too much.

Too much thinking gets you in trouble.
I shovel the food into
my bottomless pit.
I make an attempt to laugh at one of Aunt Berny's
corny jokes.
It's forced.
But I try.

quiet

It's like somebody turned down the sound
all the way.
Like somebody hit the mute button.
There's none of the city sounds I'm used to.
That constant buzz that only the city has.
Traffic, and sirens, car alarms.
Always car alarms.
Those are the sounds I'm used to.
Music to my ears.
This is like being in space or something.
No sound at all.
Nothin' except for the leaves rustling in the wind.
How do people sleep with all this

quiet.

not as bad as i thought
I'm the first one up.
Walkin' the house with my DigiTunes plastered to
my head.
Dad must have put on almost every Hendrix song
there is.
Now I can really see the place.
Not as bad as I thought, but it's still small.
I've got nothing to complain about.
We've got no place else to go.
I'm trying to tell myself that things will be okay.
I know it's a lie. But I heard
if you tell a lie long enough
it becomes the truth.
Maybe this lie will come true.
I hope it does.

1st morning
Exploring this first morning,
trying to make something out of nothing.

Everything new and not the same

as it was.
Staring
at all the smiling faces.
I feel like I could put my fist through this wall, as
Jimi screams:

> *Anger*
>
> *he smiles . . . towering—*

STOP.
Too angry to listen to this now.
Too angry to look at all these smiling faces.
What have they got to be smiling about?
Don't they know it all means nothing?
Everything we do.
And think
and
what we believe . . .
Doesn't mean a damn thing
when you can die so easily; so painfully
for nothin'.
I hit the wall

but not with my fist.

I smack it.

Smack all the smiling faces, smiling at me.

Aunt Berny and her smiling faces.

Pictures everywhere.

Friends and family

and

that one smile I don't want to see.

That one smile that hurts me.

That one smile that I must have missed last night

in the dark.

> *'Cause I'm a million miles away*
> *and at the same time I'm right here*
> *in your picture frame*

My DigiTunes is off, but I can still hear Jimi's voice.

The words pop into my head as I stare at his face.

I get that feeling again.

Deep in the pit of my stomach.

Like when the plane you're in suddenly drops

and doesn't bother to take your stomach along.

That's the feeling I have now.

The same feeling I got *that* night . . .
Staring
can't take my eyes off
that picture.
The one I didn't see before.
The one I didn't want to see.
His face
smiling back at me.

The two of us arm in arm,
smiling wide into the camera.
I wish I could jump into that picture and warn him.
Scream at him to be careful.
Scream at him not to go to the Corner.
Looking at me and Dad
in that picture frame.
I look so happy.
Happy because
I have no idea.
that
one day my dad's chest would have holes in it.
And he would die, facedown in a pool of blood.

Happy because
I have no idea that
he would never see me graduate
high school
or
college . . .
Happy because
I have no idea
that he would miss
my whole
life.

I shut my eyes and try to shake away the picture.
But it's still there.
I'm still here.

But Dad isn't.

rural
Nothin' but farms and cows
and this little town.
I'm stuck in between Fellowship and Hope.

Aunt Berny says that Hollow Falls

used to be part of Hope;

but they broke away.

Guess they lost hope.

Must be easy to do in the middle of nowhere.

the (mean) streets of hollow falls

I tuck my big 'fro underneath a baseball cap.

A leftover Cincinnati Reds cap

from the soon-to-be-forgotten-if-Aunt-Berny-has-

anything-to-do-with-it Uncle Carl days.

Everything else is all Jimi and me.

Old '60s clothes from when Dad was a kid.

Fished them out of the trunk

and made them my own.

I'm all psychedelic from the neck down.

Rainbow shirt flows over cool bell-bottom blues.

Peace-sign belt keepin' everything tight.

I go out incognito, like.

Just want to observe the town

without people observing *me*.

I cover up my "cool" attire with a long raincoat.

No rain today,

just want to play it safe in this hick town.

I walk down the driveway

and out onto Center Street.

"Just stay on Center," Aunt Berny said.

"It'll take you everyplace you want to go."

Oh, yeah? Will it take me back to the City?

I didn't think so.

Center street. At least it does what it says

it's supposed to do.

Goes right down the center of town.

I stop in at Harry's Coffee Shop.

Everyone at the counter turns and stares,

all at the same time.

Like it was some Olympic sport.

Synchronized staring or something.

The staring event continues as I order a Coke.

"Only Pepsi," the waitress says.

She doesn't even look me in the eye.

It's like she's scared of me,

like I'm too ugly to look at.

Or maybe

too black?
All white at the counter,
staring at *me*.
I take my Pepsi to go,
and walk through the rest of town.
If you could call this place a town.
The honeymoon is over already.
I don't think it ever started.
This was a big mistake.
The words rattle in my head
as I walk past the small theater.
Playing some old movie that's been out
for a year.
This one post office/one coffee shop
one hardware/grocery store
no deli havin'/sorry excuse for a
town
sucks.

voodoo chile
Almost cut my hair today
but I decided not to.

Gonna grow my 'fro out *real* big/retro-style
like Dad's used to be.
Like Jimi's.
Pick it out high.
Like they wore it in the '60s.
All afternoon, thinkin' about Jimi,
starin' at his poster
now up on my wall.
Jimi was magic, just like MAJ
just like my dad.
"Jimi operated on another plane."
Dad said that all the time.
Not the plane you fly in
another world
another universe inside of this one.
Cherokee—black—magic Jimi *burning the midnight*
lamp burning up the strings.
Changing the world.
Changing me . . .
and Jimi sings:

> *'Cause I'm a voodoo child voodoo child*
> *Lord knows I'm a voodoo child*

CHAPTER 5

acting normal

Everyone's trying to act normal.

Trying to act like me and Mom have lived here

all our lives.

Like we've lived here more than seven days.

Aunt Berny goes to work.

Mom keeps unpacking and rearranging stuff.

I just sit in my room, listening to Hendrix.

I tell Aunt Berny I like my room,

even though I hate it.

I tell Mom I'm feeling better,

even though I'm not.

I guess I lie a lot now.

I lie

but

I try to act normal. Whatever that is.

Wishing the weekend would last forever

and Monday would never come.

Wishing I didn't have to start a new school.

Gonna be September already.

At least I'll start at the beginning.

Always harder coming in the middle.

I know I'm not gonna like it here.

I know I'm not gonna like this school.

I know it.

back-to-school-shopping

Not the same without Dad to drag

around.

He hated it, but Mom made him go.

Dad would grumble and moan,

but he always helped pick out the hippest clothes.

Got me whatever I wanted.

Today we had to drive forever to get to a mall.

Stores all have stupid clothes.

Nothin' like what they got in the city.

Nothin' I want to wear.

Besides, I got my clothes now.

Mom's starting to get mad.

Doesn't take her long to get mad anymore.

Mom fades in and out.

Now she's in.

Taking it out on me.

She's tellin' me to pick something out.

Tellin' me not to be so spoiled.

Tellin' me those days are over.

Aunt Berny gives me a look,

like I should just go along with it and get something.

I bet if it was just me and Aunt Berny,

she wouldn't make me get some stupid uptight

clothes.

"These clothes suck."

I spit the words out and walk towards Pretzel Sam's.

I get what passes for a pretzel out here in

the country.

Some nasty, slimy thing.

Man, they can't even make a pretzel out here.

"We're goin' off to do some 'girl' shopping.

Meet you back here in a bit."

Aunt Berny comes over to me to see if I'm alright.

Mom doesn't. Guess she doesn't care.

I don't care either.

People are staring at me as they go by.

I don't look at them. Just look down.

Probably starin' 'cause I look different.

Not even wearin' my full-out '60s clothes.

I'm pretty toned down.

I'm sure they don't see kids who look like me.

You know, in between.

Races and times.

I'm starting to feel small.

Smaller than normal.

Dad used to say it's not how tall you are,

but how big your soul is.

Right now my soul feels tired and small,

just like me.

But the worst thing is,

this pretzel

sucks.

watchin' TV with aunt berny

"This is too scary for me.

I don't like stuff with the devil in it.

Too real for me."

Aunt Berny gets up from the couch

and walks to the kitchen.

I see her face twinge as she gets up.

She tries to hide it,

but I see it. Pain moves quickly across her face.

Arthritis in her joints. She's older than Dad.

Fifty-nine and a half. But she acts young.

Younger than Mom.

Aunt Berny says her joints have a mind of their own.

She sees what I see, and smiles.

"You can watch what you want," she says,

looking away from the TV as she walks.

"No, it's okay, I'll change it.

It's not that good anyway."

Aunt Berny comes back with a big bowl of popcorn.

Sitting in front of the TV.

Now watchin' something funny.

Just me and Aunt Berny.

Mom's asleep.

"Hey, Little Cool, so how do you like it so far?"

"Oh, it's okay, not as funny as I thought."

"No, I mean Hollow Falls?"

I pause for what seems like a lifetime.

My poker face

poked full of holes.

Aunt Berny smiles

and grabs another handful of popcorn.
"Just gonna take some getting used to,"
Aunt Berny says, answering my silence.
I'm glad I didn't have to tell her
what I was thinking.
How I wish I was anyplace but here.
How I think this is probably the worst town
in the world.
How I know I'm never gonna fit in here.
Aunt Berny's laugh changes my thoughts
like a TV clicker.
I laugh too, just because her laugh is so funny.
Like a chicken with the hiccups.
Cracks me up,
every time.

i wake with a song in my head

I know who it's for.
It's for Dad.
But the words are gone.
Lost in my dreams.
I hear the music

I can play the chords.
A cool bluesy riff, strong and
bold as love,
like Jimi says.
I think it went, hero Dad and
something, something . . . like that.
I wish I could find the words again.
I wish I could sing them out loud.
Talk to Dad through my song.
I know he would hear me.
The words just out of reach . . .
I know he would hear me.
We'd be together—
almost.
As close
as we could come.
In my room
I play his song.
Strong and bold
as
love.

sunday, church
& good riddance

Sitting in between Mom and Aunt Berny.

Scrunched on either side.

Sold-out crowd for the Lord.

So this is where all the black folks go.

Aunt Berny says it's her first time back

without Uncle Carl.

Nobody really talks about what happened

with Uncle Carl.

Like it's some kind of state secret or something.

Just a no-good dude, is what Aunt Berny says.

I thought he was okay.

He was born and raised in this town, *found that*
out.

"Never wanted to move,"

Aunt Berny said.

She just took the bad

with the good, I guess.

I never really spent a lot of time with him.

'Cause Dad never liked coming here.

He didn't like Uncle Carl too much either.

Said he wasn't honest.

Honest or not, Aunt Berny's back to the start.

Mom says she'll be fine—has a good job

and some money saved up.

Aunt Berny definitely *saved* us.

I know Mom is letting her help us.

I know Mom doesn't want to take any money from

her.

But,

I know she does.

monday-morning tie-dyed blues

Mom says: "Are you going to school like that?"

I say: "Like what?"

Mom says: "Lookin' like *that*. Did you get into your
Dad's trunk?"

I say: "You said I could have whatever was in
there."

Mom says: "I know, hon, but I don't think it's such a good idea to wear all that on your first day at a new school. These people here, they're not as, uh, open-minded as they were back home. They may not get this."

I say: "Get what? I'm just dressing how I want. It's still a free country, isn't it? Or did that end when you kidnapped me and dragged me across three states to live in this stupid hick town?"

Mom says: "What did I tell you about that mouth? You know if your dad were here, you would never talk to me like that."

I say: "Well, he's not here, is he."

don't go away mad
I hear Mom slam the car door.
Aunt Berny's old Ford
engine sputtering
just waking up, too.

Mom's got a job interview.

Outside of Columbus.

It would be a commute

but she says she'd do it.

Hope she gets it.

Mom teaches Special Ed.

Helps the kids who need a little more help.

Maybe a new job is what she needs.

Get her back on track.

Back on her feet.

Back to the way she used to be.

I shouldn't have been so harsh on her.

But sometimes I can't help it.

Sometimes, she makes me.

Never good to go away mad.

You never know if you're comin' back.

Aunt Berny's been gone since before I woke up.

I wish she was still here.

Aunt Berny *gets* me.

Gets me better than Mom. Aunt Berny's calm.

Makes me calm.

Tries to make peace when there's a fight
between me and Mom.
Aunt Berny's funny, too:
she says that hospital would shut down if it wasn't
for her.
She says it's the nurses that *really* run that place.
"Doctors are just overpaid babysitters."
Her favorite line.
Aunt Berny is so crazy sometimes.
Mom says she saves lives.

Not all of them.

like a rolling stone
In the mirror, I see:
Hendrix hat, sitting cool on top of my head,
feather and all, just like Jimi wore it.
Bandana wrapped loose around my forehead.
Big oversized tie-dyed shirt
swimming
over
army pants, pockets running down both sides,

black jacket just down to my waist.

I'll save my tricked-out velvet coat for tomorrow—

(roll the sleeves up and I'm in).

But today

I'm a psychedelic cowboy.

I pick up my six-string shooter.

Way out of tune, but I don't care.

I just want to play.

Whatever comes into my head. I just want to play.

Hand to chords.

Pick to strings—taking away some of my pain.

Nowhere to go but deeper inside.

Deeper inside,

deeper.

I start to sing one of dad's favorite songs.

"Like a Rolling Stone" by Bob Dylan,

but Jimi's version.

Quiet—in my Little Cool talkin' rasp.

A little like Hendrix and Dylan,

but mostly like me.

And the biracial boy sings:

"How does it feel baby
To be on your own
No direction home
Look at ya,
A complete unknown
Yeah, like a rollin' stone"

CHAPTER **6**

what the hell is a bobcat?
The question bounces in my brain
as I walk up the steps to the main entrance.
A giant bobcat (I guess),
snarls down at me from above.
The school colors—blue and gray, faded like some
old acid-washed jeans.
Chipped paint and a cracked window greet me
as I walk through the big double doors.
It's a good-sized school, with two floors.
Unfriendly and old-fashioned from the outside,
like an old hospital from another time.
Four grades:
Fifth, six, seventh, and eighth.
The high school is right next to it.
Stuck out here at the edge of town, out next to the
farmer's fields.
I walk down the main hallway to the office.
Have to pick up my schedule.
"Keith James."
I tell the lady my name.
It sounds strange coming out of my mouth,

like it wants to go back in.

Like my name doesn't fit here.

Like I don't fit here.

I could still make a break for it.

It's not too late.

Sprint back out the way I came.

Find some way to get out of this place.

This school/this town

this

life.

first times

Shuffling papers behind a desk.

The lady says,

"Welcome to Hollow Falls Junior High."

"Thanks," I say, my voice quivering,

like it's not sure of itself.

My stomach starts doing flips.

"Just nerves." Dad talkin' to me again,

in my head. Trying to calm me down.

He used to be real good at that.

Calmin' me down. When I was upset.

He just had a natural confidence.

It just rubbed off on you. He was always like,

"If I can do it, you can, too."

Well, Dad's not here. It's just me.

I take my schedule in my sweaty hands and walk to

my first class.

Walking slow as death, like Aunt Berny says.

Feeling cold

alone

like I'm the only one in the world.

I feel like I'm gonna throw up.

Maybe I'll puke and they'll send me home.

Tell me not to come back again.

Tell me to go back home.

My real home, back in the city.

Be fine by me.

"First times are always hard," Dad says.

"Problem is so are second and third times,"

I say back.

Me and

Dad—havin' our chat in my head.

Dad, tellin' me things will work out,

things will be okay,
just take it day by day . . .
day by
day.

First times are always hard.

first class—
attack
Old wooden desks.
Strange kids staring,
whispering under their breath.
Shaking their heads,
lookin' at me like I'm from another planet.
Have to show these kids I'm not scared.
I strut my stuff and walk to the back.
Can't even think about math.
I wish I had my axe.
Shut these kids up real fast.
Plug in my guitar, turn it up to ten.
And—
"Hey, freak, what are you supposed to be?"

The words cut my strut in half.

The whole class laughs.

I freeze and start to get dizzy.

Dad's disappeared.

Can't find him.

Now, when I need him the most.

Not in my head.

Nowhere.

Just dead.

I am **onstage**

but these lights are too bright.

Burning up my insides.

I want to cry

but that can't happen.

I can't breathe.

The air choking off.

Another panic attack.

I try to think of good things.

Dad and Mom, the way it used to be.

The past.

Breathe slowly—deep breaths.

Mrs. Davis asks if I'm okay. . . .

I nod and take a seat.
Deep breaths.
I'm okay
I'm not gonna die
I'm fine
everything's gonna be
alright.

morning waves
I ride the morning and float on top.
Trying not to drown, get swept under and slammed
onto the rocks.
Catching my breath
and sticking it out all by myself.
Classes change but
I stay the same.
Quiet.
Don't open my mouth
'cause
I don't want it to get shut.
Just keep to myself.
Until the day is done.

Until my sentence
is up.

after lunch:
captain astro-funk
"Okay class, let's settle down. You're not in seventh
grade anymore.
Let's act like the mature eighth-grade men and
women that I know you are."
Mrs. Tyler looks around the class.
Shutting kids up with her glare.
She's trying too hard.
She makes her way to the blackboard
and starts writing.
Eighth-grade English; how is it gonna be different
from seventh?
And
who cares?
My first day not even done,
and I already expect the stares.
Try to let them roll off my back,
but most stick.

Eyes slowly shift away from me and towards the
front of class.
My mind is wandering, far away from here,
back to my music, my guitar . . .
I let my mind fly high
up to another plane
where Jimi lives . . .
Words push pencil
to paper,
notes appear before my ears
and get swallowed up
and spit back out
into something
that I like,
at least for now.

> *Flying up to the stars where one day I will be*
> *Flying high to the sun I can feel its rays on me*
> *I'm Captain Astro-funk, I'll rock your soul*
> *I'm Captain Astro-funk, welcome to the show*

My hands go to the chords—C-D-G-A.
My pencil my guitar.

I could write a whole song in my head—
I could write just like Hendrix.
Right now—right here in this class.
None of these country kids would ever know.
Mrs. Tyler thinks I'm listening.
She doesn't have a clue
that I'm on another plane
in a different dimension.
I'm inside the song;
always safe
inside
the song.

the super-fine girl with the long blond hair
(quadruple take one)
"You should really take notes,
sometimes Mrs. Tyler gives pop quizzes."
The words sound like they're coming from:
a fish with a sinus condition
swimming underwater
talking on a cell phone
while driving through a tunnel.

I jump back in my seat.

I am so deep in my song

it takes me a minute to come back.

Back to the real world

back to class and this voice.

Is she talking to me?

I turn to see where the voice is coming from.

Quadruple take one:

Prettiest face I've ever seen.

Like those models on TV.

Sky-blue eyes

I can't stop staring at them.

Long blond hair falling everywhere.

I look again

and

again . . .

and

again . . .

and

again. . . .

the super-fine girl with the long blond hair
(quadruple take two)
She's a dead ringer for Cathy from back home
—Brooklyn.
The one that got away.
Actually, I never really talked to her,
so I never had the chance
to let her get away.
I walked into THE CD STOP almost every day,
just to see if she was there.
I never said anything more than "Hi."
Never said more than one word . . .
Whatever.
They could be sisters.
Except this girl looks older.
I can tell she's tall.
Taller than me. But that's easy.
Everyone's taller than me.
That is not an eighth-grade chest.
I scoot my chair back to get a closer look at
the super-fine girl with the underwater voice.

The voice definitely doesn't match the face.
Blowin' her nose
pullin' out tissues like a magician
pulling scarves from the palm of his hand.
Doesn't change a thing.
No nasty points on this girl,
nose blowin' and all.
"What?" I try to whisper but it comes out louder.
"Take   notes,"
she says in a seriously stuffed-up whisper—
blowin' her nose between words.
I pick up my pencil and pretend to take notes:
pretend I'm writing something more than
Just-My-Name.
The super-fine girl gives me a look,
like I just saved the world from destruction.
Pencil keeps slipping out of my hands.
Sweat pouring on my notebook.
Heart beating a million miles a minute.
She is *so* fine.
Her every move should be reported on the news.
They should break into all the regularly scheduled

programming

and just show her, all day, all night . . .

24/7—all the time.

She sees me and smiles.

I smile back and take the best notes

in the history of takin' notes.

Feeling so good,

knowing she's there—

the super-fine girl with the long blond hair. . . .

veronica sweet

Walking out of class, Veronica tells her tale:

Everyone calls her V. She was on vacation with her

family, got back last night.

Originally from Fort Wayne, Indiana.

Moved to Hollow Falls last year

to be closer to her Grandma Cozy.

Cozy's real name is Claire, but V's called her Cozy

ever since she can remember.

Grandma Cozy's in a nursing home in Clayton,

a couple towns over.

V's father sold his business

something to do with plastics.

V's dad doesn't *get* her. Doesn't try.

They get into lots of fights.

Don't know why . . .

V's mom doesn't work. Guess she doesn't have to.

She has one sister. Older. Name is Kate.

She's in college.

V's been to New York, but only Manhattan.

Never to Brooklyn.

She loves New York, she says.

I'm downloading V's life story into my head as fast
as I can.

Blown away that she's actually talking to me.

Blown away that this super-fine girl would even
want to talk to me.

Blown away.

silent rage

"*Need something, hippie?*

Didn't think so."

The words sting, but not as much

as what comes after.

Standing in front of my locker.

Alone. Veronica's gone.

Waiting for these big corn-fed lookin' dudes to move
out of the way.

POWERS and

COLES.

Your typical eighth-grade Neanderthals.

Big red letters on the back of oversized jerseys.

Powers looks like the Incredible Hulk—

except he's not green—

his shirt about to burst at the seams.

Some kind of eighth-grade monster created in a lab
or something.

Buzz cut/big arms/big everything.

Both of them way too big for their age;

probably flunked anyway.

They stare at me, hard and mean,

like they hate me.

They don't even know me.

But I can feel their hate

and smell their nasty country breath.

They're trying to intimidate me.

Trying to make me scared.

I am scared—but I really need my history book.

Seventh period's gonna start soon.

Now they go into ignore mode,

back to their stupid conversation,

acting like I'm not even here.

Like I don't exist.

That's what hurts the most.

Trying to stand tall,

but

that's hard when you're me.

The good feeling I just had

with V

gone so fast.

RAGE TAKES ME BY SURPRISE

but only on the inside.

I want to scream at them.

I want to hit them

and kick them, Jackie-Chan style

and

make them hurt as much as

I
do.
To cry
like I cry.
I want to have the power
for once.
To be in control
for once.
Dad always said, "Peace and love,"
but look what that got him.
RAGE BUILDS
inside my head;
but I've got
nothin' to back it up.
Not even some guts.
I don't even look the big dudes in the eye.
I just walk away,
without my books;
without my pride,

without.

45 seconds later

I take out my DigiTunes and try to escape this place

myself.

I push back the tears and concentrate on

my big feet, moving my little legs

up these stupid steps.

Why am I such a crybaby? Can't let these kids see.

Can't give them more of a reason to hate me.

On the way to seventh period, history.

I hear Jimi sing:

> *Let me stand next to your fire*
> *Let me stand next to your fire*
> *Oh, let me stand*

I feel hot, from Hendrix riffs and

the stuffy second-floor heat.

I watch as everyone starts filing in.

I wait until the last kid goes into class.

I want to keep Jimi playin' as long as I can.

as long as I got Jimi I'm okay.

"Are we in or out?"

Mr. Porter gives me a smile.

I look at him,

his hands, big and rough,

calluses in all the right spots.

I bet teaching isn't his only gig.

"I'm in."

history

"Hey, Little Cool, why don't ya come help me with

this mix."

Dad's big hands

floating over his ProControl mixing board.

A ballet with fingers and knobs.

Raising up the bottom-end bass,

adding a little treble top.

Once he gets it like he wants,

then the computer takes over.

I sit down, right next to him.

Dad lets me help program the moves.

"Drop in the guitar solo after 2nd chorus.

Add keyboards.

Don't forget the harmonies."

I can almost smell the studio.

A mixture of sweet and sweat and

newly painted walls.

"Little Cool, get ready.

You know what I always say,

one bad mix can kill a career.

Mine."

Dad's smile taking up the whole room.

Laughing his silly high-pitched laugh.

My dad the producer.

He's the one that makes you bob your head.

He's the one that makes you sing along.

He's the one—

"So, Keith, what do you think?"

Mr. Porter's voice snatches me from the past,

and back to history class.

I have no idea what he's talking about.

No idea what's going on.

I scratch my head, and pat my 'fro,

pretending I know the answer.

Really, I'm just stalling for time.

Hoping for a fire drill.

Hoping for anything.

I feel stares and smirks,

and pressure on my back.

Time stops and the clock is ticking.

I should have *never* gotten out of bed this morning.

walking out of school

My first day

finally done.

I'm trying to make a fast exit into the weekend.

"I like how you dress."

The underwater voice makes me turn clear around.

I am stunned.

Veronica Sweet is talking to me

AGAIN.

I had convinced myself

she was just being nice before.

Just talking to me because she felt sorry for me.

The super-fine girl being nice to the short, weird kid

with the dead dad. (Does she know?)

I've seen it in the movies all the time.

Happens in real life, too.

It's happened to me.

Back home in Brooklyn.

I become someone's *friend*, their little pet.

Forget that mess,

won't let that happen again.

But this girl is off the hook.

Off the chain

off

everything.

V is waiting for me to answer her

as the herd of kids pushes past.

"Thanks," I hear myself say.

"See ya later," I think I hear her say.

She likes how I dress.

How I dress.

"See ya,"

I finally say to the back of her head,

which is also super-fine.

She moves fast, but fast is good.

Fast is *definitely,*

good.

"Watch where you're goin', hippie."

I feel some kid's shoulder dig into me.
But I don't mind; it doesn't bother me, now.
I flash the peace sign and take a bow.
The whole student body my sold-out crowd.
V erases all the bad from the day
with one smile.
With just a few words.
With just
her.
I'm Keith James;
you've been great.
See ya next time.
God bless and

Good night.

CHAPTER 7

small town

Three weeks gone in this stupid small town.

Stupid small minds . . .

big accusing eyes,

starin' at me like I stole somethin'.

It's like I'm guilty.

Guilty as charged.

Every time me and Mom go to the store,

the checkout girl is always checkin' *me*,

checkin' me out to see

if I'm not hidin' something under my coat.

Give me a break.

They don't know we're together.

So;

Mom shoots her one of her patented:

Don't even think about messin' with us

superhard mom stares.

The checkout girl goes back to ringing us up,

quick.

What's wrong?

Hasn't anyone around here seen:

a caramel face–lookin' kid

with a big bushy 'fro
wearin' a psychedelic cowboy hat,
multicolored bell bottoms,
and a rainbow shirt—
walkin' with a gray-haired middle-aged white lady?

I guess not.

gray
Walking through town after school
doesn't take very long.
If you blink, you might miss Hollow Falls,
but that wouldn't be a bad thing.
I wish we would have blinked.
This one-stoplight town
(okay, maybe there's two)
is always gray.
It's just depressing.
Everything about it is gray.
The houses and streets and even the people are gray.
Like they have a coating on them.
Always dusty.

Sidewalks roll up by seven o'clock.

I hate this town.
Hate the people, too.
I can hear what they say when I pass them.
No, they are not more polite out in the country.
Talkin' junk like: *"hippie,"* and *"weirdo,"*
"It's not Halloween,"
and
"What are you supposed to be?"
under their breath,
but just over it enough for me to hear.
Dumb people shake their heads when I walk by.
Like I don't belong here.
Well, they're right.
I don't.
But I can't do anything about it.
So, too bad.
If it's too bad for me/then it's too bad for you.
Walking past Harry's Place,
getting angrier with each step,
I watch a row of gray folks at the counter.

Probably talkin' about stupid gray stuff.

Drinkin' their gray coffee.

Livin' their gray lives. . . .

The sun is starting to slide off now.

Dropping fast.

Even the sun doesn't like to stay too long

in this town.

Probably has somewhere better to be.

I want to take the next bus out of this town.

The next plane.

The next something . . .

I wish I was back home.

I would give anything to be,

back home.

gnawing at me

How could we almost be put out on the street?

What if we didn't have Aunt Berny?

Where would we have lived?

Questions gnawing at me before I fall asleep.

I hear late-night talks. I hear what they say

when they think I'm sleeping.

I can hear them talking in this little house.

Late at night.

trying to figure it out

but

they don't know.

Why: The mortgage hadn't been paid in months.

Why: The savings was just about gone.

Why: The money seemed like

it just disappeared.

Why: There's so many unpaid bills . . .

Late-night worries and unanswered questions:

"Why is it taking so long for that insurance to

come?"

"Are you sure we changed the address?"

and "What if the check got lost in the mail?"

"We need that money to live;

you know I didn't get that job, Berny,

so many bills

all of mine and his too.

Credit cards and—Berny,

we need that money, to survive."

Mom's words making me sick.

My stomach falls down into my feet.

Dropping fast;

like being stuck upside down on the Crazy Eight.

Queasy—again.

Mom says times were getting tough in the music biz,

but she still thought Dad

was doing fine.

"Always hurts the little guy first," Aunt Berny says.

I didn't know Dad was a little guy.

I guess he used to be bigger.

"Times change fast," Aunt Berny says.

Times change fast.

no blood
(that you can see)

Week two in this dumb country school.

Keep to myself.

Keep everyone else

away.

Far away as possible.

But sometimes it's not that easy.

Sometimes they get too close:

"Why don't you go back where you came from?"

"Nobody wants you here."

"Go back to New York where they like them freak-
shows comin' to town."

Right up in my face.

Don't know their names.

Don't want to anyway.

In the hallway

in between classes

kids pass me by

hitting me with hate

for no reason.

Words like bullets

but without the mess.

No blood that you can see.

My bell-bottom blues dragging

on the pea-green tiles.

I listen to Jimi and

try to block *them* out.

>   . . . *People try to pull me down*
>   *They talk about me like a dog*

Talkin about the clothes I wear
But they don't realize they're the ones
   who's square

If Dad was here it would be different.
They wouldn't say those things to me.
They would know better.
Dad would have my back
and I wouldn't
keep walking.
I'd be.

   Stone free
   do what I please
   Stone free
   to ride the breeze
   Stone free
   I can't stay;
   I gotta, gotta, gotta get away

not just another pretty face
The end of Week Three;
and

V

has a lot to say

about a lot of things.

She's like a city girl

trapped in the country.

We agree on most things.

How crazy things are

and how our country is

being flushed down the drain.

"I wouldn't have voted for him," she says.

"You know I wouldn't have," I say back.

Trying to feel her out

see if she's for real.

For now she seems race-less.

She doesn't see in colors like

most folks around here seem to do.

"Now, my parents, well, that's another story.

Sometimes they're too conservative. Guess that's just

how they were raised." V sounds like she's

apologizing for them. She gives me a look

like she's saying *she's* not her parents.

"My mom, well, at least she has an open mind.

Can't say that about my dad. I don't really get along
with him.
You'd think with my dad's business and all—
travelin' all over—he'd be more open-minded.
Sometimes I hate the way he talks.
Can't believe the things that come out of his
mouth."
V stops short, like she was gonna keep talking.
She looks at me
like she thinks she's said too much.
Looking at me kind of sideways
not sure of what I'm gonna say.
I don't say anything.
I just let it go.
I don't really want to hear any more.
I'm just glad V's not like her dad;
I'm just really glad of that.

and she likes jimi too

V's heard of Jimi, knows a few tunes.
Just the most popular ones; like "Purple Haze."

I tell her about Jimi and his Band of Gypsys.
And before that, Jimi Hendrix and the Experience:
the great drumming of Mitch Mitchell,
and how Noel Redding laid down the bass,
gave Jimi a foundation to build his
"Red House" on.
I tell her all about
his short life—
from the blues to
Jupiter. Jimi took the guitar to another level.
Another universe.
I let V listen to some tunes.
Between classes.
Lunchtime, too.
She's getting hooked,
I can tell.
Moving to Jimi's groove,
just like I do.
Her hair falls into her face; she starts to shake
everything; from top to bottom
and back again.

i love how

V's face lights up and

her eyes get wide when I talk.

Not just about Jimi, but about anything.

Like she really wants to know.

It's not just that she's fine—super-fine, I mean.

I could watch her jeans forever. . . .

Don't want to even start on her chest.

Actually I wish I could—

She drives me craaaazy.

But what puts her over the top

is that she listens.

See, that's the coolest thing.

She listens.

To me.

She

wants

to

hear . . .

what

I

have to

say. . . .

not ready yet

Most kids know that my dad is dead.

Word travels fast in a small town.

Veronica knows, too.

We don't really talk about it.

I can tell she wants to know more about him.

Not how he died, but how he lived.

What he did.

Kind of not what I was expecting her

to want to know.

But it's a nice surprise.

Still, I don't say much.

Just that he was in the music business.

Too hard for me to get into it,

at least out loud.

Too hard for me to relive.

For now,

it's just too hard.

the truth is. . .

waiting for something bad to happen.

Always waiting for something bad to happen.

Aunt Berny says it's called heightened vigilance.

When you have a trauma or tragedy you always

think something bad's gonna happen so you don't

want to be surprised.

If you're always ready for

the next terrible thing to happen

then you won't be surprised.

I don't want another surprise.

I call it living on the edge of your seat.

That's what it feels like to me. . . .

I watch V eat her salad

she's even sexy when she chews.

"So what's your mom like?"

V asks, smiling.

Her white teeth almost blinding me.

I tell her what she was, not what she is.

". . . Funny, a pretty cool mom . . . and can throw

down in the kitchen."

I hear the words coming out of my mouth, knowing

they're not true.

But I say them anyway.

The truth is:

Mom barely smiles anymore;

hasn't cooked in ages.

I don't even know what my mom is like anymore.

The truth is:

I don't even know. . . .

bad vibes

every time me and V are together.

Tryin' to figure us out.

I can feel the bad vibes.

The hate getting stronger every day.

Especially from that Powers kid.

The Hulk.

He looks like he wants to kill me.

His looks—getting stronger and stronger,

longer and longer.

I don't tell V.

She doesn't need to know.

Just as long as I see it comin'

I'll be okay.

Just as long as I

see it comin'. . . .

canceled

"What the hell is this?

Canceled? Lack of payment?

You mean he stopped paying the life insurance

premiums?

Isn't it enough that you're dead?

Do I have to suffer more?

Do I have to just keep suffering?"

Mom is yelling at the air.

Yelling at the piece of paper she's holding.

Yelling at Dad.

Aunt Berny's not home yet.

Mom's talking to that piece of paper.

Some kind of letter from the insurance company.

Now she's waving it in the air.

Waving and talking at the same time.

Mom runs into her bedroom.

Then runs back out carrying a green metal box.

Drawers almost coming out—she's moving fast.
Mom puts the box in the middle
of the living-room floor.
Pulling out drawers and papers.
Looking for something,
I don't even think she knows.
Maybe just trying to do something to make herself
feel better.
I watch Mom pick up a key with a yellow tag
off the floor.
She's staring at it, staring at that little yellow tag.
Like it's some rock
that the Mars Explorer brought back.
Completely foreign to her.
She keeps staring; I hear her say something
but I don't know what. A low mumble
that I can't make out.
Then she puts the key in her sweatpants pocket.
"Everything's supposed to be in this box.
I always saw you looking for stuff in here,
down in that studio.
I should have paid more attention.

I really should have. . . .

Here's the policy.

This is what I used when I filed the claim.

How can they say it's canceled?

Why didn't you pay it, MAJ?

What happened to all the money?"

Her voice is getting loud again, filling up the room.

"We needed that money.

That fifty grand was already spent.

I have collection agencies on my back.

Why did you do this to me?"

Now it's getting worse.

More than just talking out loud.

Mom is having a conversation with

Dad, just like he was standing next to her.

And

she's totallly unaware

that I am in the living room,

sitting on the couch

watching TV.

I feel my chest tightening

and my breath running away.

I try to pretend I don't hear her.

Try to drown her out with my DigiTunes.

But I don't have the volume up.

I want to hear what's going on.

I want to hear Mom.

mom sees me

She sees the look on my face.

Sees that I'm upset.

Scared.

Starting to lose my breath.

"It's okay, I'll get to the bottom of this.

Don't worry. It's going to be okay. It's just a mistake,

just some red tape I have to cut through.

It's going to be alright.

Don't get upset. Everything's going to work out.

We'll be alright."

Mom says the words, but she's not convincing.

It's like she's reading from a script.

Just delivering lines to try to keep me calm.

To keep me from having another panic attack.

Mom pats me on the top of my head

and walks to her bedroom,
slower this time, careful not to let the drawers fall
out of the box.
Acting like everything's alright.
I guess she did her job.
A few words and a pat on the head.
That's supposed to make everything okay.
That's supposed to take away what I saw.
That look on her face—
that scared me more than what I heard.
She looked like she was going to just die right then
and there.
Like she was just going to give up.
Like she just couldn't take
one
more
thing.

me and aunt berny pretending
Me and Aunt Berny and the Sunday-night movies.
Mom shuffles into the kitchen
to get a drink of water.

When did she start shuffling like an old lady?

She gives a weak wave and keeps on moving.

All the way back to her room.

Mom in her room.

Since yesterday,

she's been in her room or on the phone.

Talking to that insurance company

and her lawyer back home.

A friend of Mom's who's helping us out.

Aunt Berny comes closer on the couch.

This is like our ritual now.

Movies and popcorn.

And a lot of pretending.

Pretending it isn't weird that Mom isn't with us.

Pretending we're not worried that Mom

is shutting down.

Pretending that we're not thinking about Dad.

About MAJ.

About all those

bullets.

Aunt Berny smells like a doctor's office.

That sickly sweet disinfectant smell.

She worked a double today at the hospital.

She's working more and more lately,

weekends, too.

Aunt Berny looks tired.

She lets out a quiet moan,

almost like a whisper,

as she shifts her weight on the couch.

Her arthritis, acting up.

She still has a smile on her face.

Aunt Berny's always in a good place.

Brings the love wherever she goes.

I'm starin' at the TV but my mind is on V.

On tomorrow, Monday.

The whole thing starts all over again.

I hate that school/the kids/the classes.

But V saves me.

She saves the day.

Can't wait to talk to her again.

I know, I'm takin' the bait,

might get hurt bad in the end.

But for now,

it feels good

just to be around her.

I know I'm takin' the bait;

but

I just can't help myself. . . .

CHAPTER 8

every morning
this is what I do.

I get to school before first bell.

Go to my locker.

Get to the bathroom right as first bell buzzes.

Then I check my self out.

Make sure the 'fro is just right.

My nose doesn't look too big.

My shirt is at its utmost psychedelic-ness.

'Cause right after first period, I see V.

I can usually time it perfectly

so I'm walking past her class

as she's walking out.

Then first period starts,

and I can't wait for it to end.

So far we're just friends

but

I pretend me and Veronica are together.

Like a *real* couple.

Like boyfriend and girlfriend.

Walking hand in hand,

arm in arm

down the halls.

Mrs. Davis writes a problem on the board—

but I am with V.

I'm not really sitting in this seat.

In this class,

in this school.

I can stare at Mrs. Davis and nod,

like I'm following along.

But really

I am following Veronica's jeans.

One hand inside her right back pocket.

Holding her as close as I can.

every night

I take out my electric and play.

Headphones into my practice mini-amp;

I'm ready to

J

a

m.

Step on my distortion pedal and feel the rush.

Feel the fuzz,

feel the buzz running through my body.

Like an electric current that doesn't shock,

just rocks your insides OUT.

I grabbed some of Dad's gear,

small stuff that Mom wouldn't know about.

I can play an E chord and sound like a

ROCK GOD.

I plug into the box that says,

Maj Effects 1

The Majinator,

press "on" and the LED lights

go wild.

I am a "Voodoo Chile,"

blasting off to another world.

Where bad things

don't happen.

Where people

don't get shot for buying a Diet Coke.

I feel close to Dad when I play.

Touching the stuff that he touched.

That he used every day.

I fall to my knees like Jimi did

and recite my nightly prayers:
All praises
to
Page
and
Clapton
and
Beck
to
Jimi Almighty
all
powerful.
Give me the strength
to kick ass
and take names,
so that one day,
I can play like you
and be
like you,
on top of the world,
a star that shines bright
forever

and

never

burns

out.

does she like me?

You'd think I'd know, right?

After a month and a half?

But I don't.

I never know if someone likes me.

Especially someone as fine as V.

Why would she like me, anyway?

Veronica Sweet.

Even her last name says what she is.

Sweet.

She's the reason I get out of bed in the morning.

She's the one that keeps me going.

I know I like her.

But does she like me?

Me and V.

Little Cool, with my big 'fro,

and the super-fine blond bombshell.

Now *that* would be sweet.

stirrin' the pot

Sometimes just me and Aunt Berny are home.

Just the two of us.

Aunt Berny in the kitchen, making her famous chili.

The smell, distracting me from my homework.

I watch Aunt Berny work her magic over the stove.

A dash of this and that.

Using the big spoon like she's playing an instrument.

Humming softly as she stirs.

Aunt Berny wants to ask me something,

I can tell. She's got that look.

We are quiet in the kitchen

listening to the sound

of the chili beginning to bubble.

"So, Little Cool, how are things going?"

Aunt Berny stirrin' in the question with

the chili powder. She asks easy

as she puts the top back on the pot.

But the answer is hard.

Almost going on two months—too long, in this

place.

I miss home.

I miss The City.

I want to tell her about V.

But what would I say?

Aunt Berny's done so much for us.

I don't want to tell the truth,

too much truth these days,

too much reality, anyway.

"It'll get better," she says with a smile.

Aunt Berny reading my mind again.

Didn't even need to say a word.

That's just her.

sweat

rolling down my neck.

She sits down,

takes out her perfectly wrapped

turkey-and-whatever sandwich.

She hasn't mentioned Friday night.

What do I say? Is it really a date?

I mean, she said,

"Let's go to the movies Friday night.

Check out *Evil Dawn*

now.

Then we can see

it again, in two weeks. Halloween night."

That's two dates, right?

I said, "Great." I think I said great.

What did I say? I have no idea.

I know I said yes.

But is it really a date?

Maybe that's just what she says to everyone.

Like, to make conversation.

You know—

"How's it goin'? Classes goin' good?

How's the family?

Hey, let's go to the movies Friday night."

I try to keep my poker face.

I take a bite of my burger,

and then another.

Nervous eating is better than nervous talking.

How does she eat without getting

anything on her face?

Small talk is even smaller when you're

five-foot-nothin'.

But I hold my own.

She gets up and starts to turn away.

"My mom said she would take us on Friday."

Silence from my end.

Maybe my signal faded.

"Keith, hello?

Day after tomorrow? Friday?

The *movies*?"

"I know, cool, sounds good.

I was just thinkin' about a test I have."

Good save.

"I bet you were."

Her smile makes my chest tighten.

Makes it harder to breath.

But in a good way.

A VeronicAttack.

Now I can't eat.

All I can do is think about me and V

at the movies Friday night.

In this moment there is nothing wrong,

everything is right with the world.

I have just won the Lotto.

I am six foot two

and

my band just sold out twelve nights in a row

at Madison Square Garden.

V—minus 56 hours, 13 minutes, 45 seconds

and

counting . . .

make that 43 seconds . . .

41 seconds . . .

40 seconds . . .

39 . . .

38 . . .

37 . . .

hip-hop high, yeah, right

These kids are a trip at this school.

White country kids thinkin' they're from

South Central L.A.

All of them sittin' together at lunch.

Tryin' to be gangstas.

Tupac is rolling over in his grave.

Sometimes it's cool being in the middle like me.

I get to see both sides.

Sometimes it's clearer in the middle.

Sometimes it's not.

Right now, there's not a cloud in the sky.

Only a few black kids in this school,

but even they act like

the white kids

tryin' to act like

black kids

who grew up in "the 'hood."

Now that's just wrong.

I think they need to make an announcement

over the PA:

"Attention wannabe gangstas

of Hollow Falls Junior High

You are not 50 Cent.

You are not DMX.

You are not Ice Cube.

Get a life or

you'll all be expelled.

Thank you and have a great day.
(BIAAATCH . . .)

thursday
(the day before)
Sitting in class.
Waiting for the day to end.
Going so slow, probably on purpose, to torture me.
Bells buzz—but I can't hear them.
Teacher's words have no meaning.
The only thing I can think of is tomorrow night.
That's it.
I'm feelin' good.
For the first time
in a
l
o
n
g
time.
Dad would say I was "da man,"
goin' out with a girl like V.

Yeah, he would say I was definitely,
"da man."

walking home from school
my big feet never touch the ground.
I am floating above these gray sidewalks
and over the flat cornfields.
Watching the farmers harvesting their crops.
On my way to the *Sweet* promised land.
Each step bringing me closer to Friday night.
My date with V.
Yes, it's a date.
It has to be.
A *real* date.
I take out my DigiTunes
and scroll to my "Jimi" playlist.
I sing along with Jimi.
He sings along with me:

> *You got me floatin' round and round*
> *You got me floatin . . .*

I should have been watching where I was going.

I should have been watching who was sneaking up

behind me.

I should have seen it comin'. . . .

this is what I heard:

"What you got to be singin' about, hippie?

You know everyone thinks you're a joke.

You really think you're gonna' be with Veronica?

You really think even if she did like you,

we'd let you two be together?

You think we'd let that happen?

Let someone like you ruin our school.

Poison our girls with your . . .

whatever you are.

What are you anyway?"

"Mixed breed, is what they call 'em."

"Is that what you are? Some kind of mixed breed?

You tryin' to be white, aren't you?

Wearin' those stupid hippie clothes.

Tryin' to cover up what you really are.

I bet you don't even know what you are,

do you?

Well, let me tell you what you are.

You're just a little black runt with a dead daddy.

Oh yeah, we heard about that."

"Probably a gang shooting."

"Was your daddy in a gang? I bet he was."

"All of 'em are in gangs, either gangs or jail."

"Well, you listen here.

We've got no use for your freaky mixed-up family.

Maybe you and your white momma

might just think about livin' someplace else.

Maybe you should think about relocatin'.

Might be good for your health,

if ya know what I mean?

Bet you don't feel like singin' now, do ya?

No, didn't think so.

You have a nice rest of the day, ya hear . . .

and don't forget our little talk."

this is what i said:

Nothing.

CHAPTER 9

bobby powers

I want to say it out loud.

Scream it into the living room.

I want to punch something.

I want to cry. I want to hurt—

I want . . .

my dad back.

I can feel my eyes getting full.

I run to the bathroom.

Out of sight of Aunt Berny and Mom.

They lower the TV and ask what's wrong.

I don't answer.

I keep going, straight into the bathroom.

Lock the door. Turn on the water.

Can't catch my

breath.

I breathe deep and

slow.

I reach into my pocket and grab my pills.

I look at the label—Prescriber: FRANKS, MICHAEL P.

TAKE ONE TABLET TWICE A DAY AS NEEDED.

Dr. Franks. Saw him once before we moved.

He told me to try to take it easy.

What kind of medical advice is that?

I'm supposed to see the school counselor

once a week.

But I don't.

What's he gonna do for *me*?

I start to get even more mad.

At Powers, and Mom for being so far.

Mad at Dad for leaving me without any defense.

Now, just ripe for the pickin's,

like they say out here.

Don't want Mom and Aunt Berny hearing me catch

my breath.

Better to try to stop it before it gets bad.

I swallow a pill and stare into the mirror.

My eyes are red.

I try to shake away the tears.

Pushing them away; pushing as hard as I can.

I try to make my mind blank.

I don't want to let any thought in.

Friend or foe.

I don't want to think, about anything.

It doesn't work.

Bobby Powers—his face in my head.

His face is all I see. Evil freckles, and a buzz cut.

His upper lip twitching/out of control.

Snuck up on me with that stupid walk.

Creepin along, slow,

like a predator stalking his prey.

Stalking me.

gone

Powers and Coles.

Should have seen it comin'.

Knew it was comin'.

Got too distracted with V.

Got in the way of my street smarts.

Seemed like they just came out of nowhere.

Out of the gray, they just appeared.

The second wave tries to attack.

Reserve tears called up, ready for action.

A couple get through my perimeter,

but I fight the rest back.

I turn the water on stronger, then weaker,

trying to cover up the sound of my tears.

I blow my nose and flush.

I should have punched those rednecks.

Nobody talks to me like that.

Why didn't I punch them?

Why didn't I at least *say* something?

Dad would've been so mad that I

didn't at least say something.

He always taught me to stand up for myself.

Why did I freeze?

What's wrong with me?

Mom knocks and asks if I'm alright.

Am I alright?

I haven't been alright since that night.

The night Dad died.

He didn't just die.

He was killed.

Died, just sounds like it was natural causes.

Some kind of accident.

Dad didn't die of natural causes.

It was caused, on purpose.

It was caused by

too many bullets ripping up his chest.

And now he's gone.

Left me alone.

Alone.

Mom is knocking again.

She probably just needs to use the bathroom.

I can hear her and Aunt Berny talking—

trying to keep their voices down.

I sit down on the cold bathroom floor.

Knees up close to my chin.

I feel sad and lost.

And dumb.

Beat up, too.

Even though those rednecks

never laid a hand on me.

I feel like I lost. A lot—today,

that night.

Myself.

What I was.

What I am.

Gone in one day.

Gone in one night.

Gone.

tossing and turning

and there is no good side.

My room is dark and I feel like Dad is far.

Maybe he's jammin' with Jimi

up on that big stage

in heaven.

Tossing and turning,

and sleep is as far away as Dad.

I have to get my rest for my big date.

Gotta look good for V.

I have to sleep.

I have to go to sleep.

I can see Bobby Powers's face when I close my eyes.

I can see *his* hate and *my* fear.

I can feel my shame.

It makes my stomach turn.

Like spoiled milk.

My eyes get heavy.

I want to sleep, but I don't want to miss Dad.

He might make it back from his gig.

Might make it back before I fall asleep.

I don't wanna miss him.

I don't wanna miss.

punk

I wanted to say I was sick

but Mom would never let me go out tonight.

Neither would Aunt Berny.

I walk the halls like the floors are filled with

land mines.

I keep my head low, take all my books with me to

every class.

Don't stop at my locker once.

Don't go to the bathroom once.

I skip lunch and sit in the library.

I feel like a punk for being scared.

I feel like a punk for not standing up for myself.

I feel like

a

punk.

friday night at the movies

"I love scary movies, don't you?

I heard this was supposed to be *real* scary.

Mona and Patty said it was real good too.

I think you're gonna like it."

I nod and smile, but my mind is someplace else.

First, thinkin' about Mona and Patty,

two of V's friends.

They always pretend they don't see me

when I pass them in the halls, but I know they do.

Just barely polite when me and V are together.

I look at V, her lips shiny with butter from

the popcorn.

I should be holdin' V's hand,

and kissin' those buttery lips

and

makin my move. . . .

Instead, I keep looking out for Bobby Powers,

and his goon, Coles. They got into my head.

Into my soul.

Now they're ruining my date.

I try to talk, lay down my rap.

But it comes out all wrong.

All lame. All flat.

V is telling me about all the cool places she's been.

Traveling all over with her family.

It's like she worked for the travel channel
or something.

"You should go to Italy.

The food is the best in the world.

They have pastas in shapes that you've never even
seen before.

And it's so-o-o goood."

V is talking in between handfuls of popcorn and
slurps of Diet Coke.

"Germany is cool, too.

We were in Berlin for a whole summer once.

My dad had a plastics plant there.

It's a real cool city. It's kinda like New York,
but with lakes and a lot more space."

V is getting more and more amped up on the
Diet Coke
and Choco-lots.

Talking faster and faster.

Not much room for me to talk.

That's okay.

Don't really feel much like talking anyway.

Her family's got money.

Lots of money.

We had money once.

We used to travel too.

But then my dad got murdered and that was that.

Everything changed.

Fast.

The movie starts

I try to stop my thoughts.

Try to be in the moment.

Try to be with V.

I try to watch the screen

but

all I see is real life:

Powers and Coles

and

Dad's chest exploding all over the deli floor.

I look over at V, she's got a big smile on her face

but she's definitely on her side.

No spillage into my seat.
No spillage at all.
I should take her hand
squeeze it tight.
Does she want me to?

mom is waiting
right inside the door.
I can see her from the driveway.
"Who's that?" Veronica's mom says,
pulling up to the house.
"That's my mom," I answer quick,
pulling at the latch,
trying desperately to get out of the car,
before this goes any further.
"Here, let me help." Veronica leans over
and pulls the latch up,
opening the door.
"Thanks for driving us, Mrs. Sweet," I say,
still trying to make a fast exit.
Veronica's mom pauses before she answers,
her eyes glued to my mom

standing at the front door.

She looks confused.

Didn't think a brown kid could have a white mom,
huh?

"You're welcome, Keith," she finally says.

Veronica jumps out of the big SUV.

I follow—both of us standing in the glare of the
headlights.

"Did you like the movie?" Veronica asks.

"Yeah, it was cool." I'm looking down,
the lights too bright in my eyes.

"I told you you were gonna like it.

Well, see ya Monday."

"Yeah, see ya."

I look over my shoulder and Veronica is jumping
back into the SUV,
her ponytail bouncing up and down.

That's not all that's bouncing.

Now I'm more confused than V's mom.

I mean, what's up with us?

I still don't know if that was a date,
or was she just taking her new pet out for the night?

Inside

Mom is gone.

Everything is quiet.

Aunt Berny is sitting on the couch reading

one of those romance novels with the big bright

orange sunset on the cover.

I walk past her on my way upstairs.

"Must have been a good date, huh?" Aunt Berny

asks, giving me a sly smile.

I don't say a word. I give Aunt Berny the same smile

and keep on walkin'.

Still not knowin' what the hell happened tonight.

Still not knowin' what the hell is up

with me and

V.

rewinding the night

before bed.

I guess it wasn't as bad as I thought.

(Or maybe it was.)

I tried to lay down my Little Cool rap. Got better as

the night went on.

After the movie, waiting for her mom,
we talked.
A little more back and forth.
A little less just V.
I think we were both more relaxed.
Maybe she was waiting for me to make
the first move.
Man, I hope I didn't blow it.

the dream

Always the same.
Dad walks in,
puts his money on the counter.
Cash register rings
then everything turns red.
The sound
of
slow-motion
shouts and threats
then
bullet blasts burning holes
in his chest.

Burning holes

with fire

and

blood

fire

and

blood.

Fire

and

blood.

same as before

Almost two weeks since our date

and nothin's changed.

I thought the date was cool,

V said so too.

But we're still the same as before.

SAME AS BEFORE

Friends

and

nothing more.

what does all this mean?

Tomorrow's Halloween

and I wish this was a trick.

Definitely not a treat.

Coming home from school

just shutting the door

I walk into the living room

just in time to see Mom

fall

onto the couch.

Hard.

Dropping papers everywhere.

I run to try to break her fall

but I'm too late.

She bounces off pillows and cushions, collapsing.

Legs sprawled onto the floor. Half on the couch—

twisted.

Like this world I've been thrown into.

Twisted . . .

Aunt Berny splashes water on Mom's face

and speaks in soothing tones.

I try to hold her hand.

Her eyes are closed but she's not asleep.

Just temporarily checking out.

"What's going on?"

My voice barely able to make its way

out of my mouth.

Aunt Berny just looks at me and shakes her head.

I scoop up the papers off the floor and read

the letter on top;

something from the lawyer back home.

Something about the contents

of a safety-deposit box.

Bank statements

and other documents

I don't know what.

I see the key with the yellow tag on the floor,

on the other side of the room,

wedged up against the baseboards,

like someone threw it.

"What's going on, what does all this mean,

what's wrong with Mom?"

I feel like I can't breathe.

Aunt Berny comes over and hugs me.

Tears streaming from her eyes . . .
Tears welling up in mine and
I don't even know why.

another life

Mom is in her room. Aunt Berny gave her something
to calm her down
and make her sleep.
But now Aunt Berny is talking;
telling me this is something I need to know.
"I don't believe in hiding things.
Even the bad. That's life, it's gonna be full
of the good and full of the bad. But hiding things
isn't gonna make the bad any better. No sir.
I'm sorry Little Cool, I'm so sorry . . ."
Aunt Berny giving an intro into the bad news.
Bad news doesn't need an intro.
Just tell it.
Just tell it.
Bad-news bombs start to explode,
Aunt Berny telling me things
I really don't want to hear. . . .

My father had another bank account.

Full of money.

Money he deposited over the years.

Money from his music—when times were good . . .

but

also money he took from us—when times were not

so good. . . .

Wire transfers and withdrawals.

Taking money from our family

and giving it to

another

woman. . . .

Some name I've never heard of.

Someone I now hate

more than anyone else in the world.

"That account used to be full of money,"

Aunt Berny says.

Now it's all gone. Everything spent; sent to

that "other woman." Aunt Berny can barely speak.

Trying to talk like she's talking about someone else.

Not her own flesh and blood.

Not her own brother.

"Little Cool, there's something else you need to know."

Aunt Berny hands me a piece of paper.

I'm trying to focus on the words.

But it's hard through the tears.

My heart is beating fast,

still trying to catch my breath. . . .

I feel sick and scared

and dizzy all at the same time.

Aunt Berny is telling me to take one of my pills.

But I can't do anything except stare at that name.

He even spelled it the same way.

How come that's not *my* name?

Didn't Dad love me as much?

I start to get mad.

No, this is way more than mad.

This is something I've never felt

before.

Beyond mad

at

Dad

for dying

and lying

and cheating

and leaving us

with nothing

but

pain

and

tears.

My hands are shaking and I feel like I'm going to

pass out.

I still can't believe what I've heard.

What I've read,

reading now, with my own eyes—staring

at the top of the page/reading those two words

over and over again.

Birth Certificate

My eyes scrolling down

the page.

Scrolling down with hate

and rage

and

shock.

My world turned inside out

again

and again

and again.

DENISE CORA JACOBS—MOTHER

MARVIN ANTHONY JAMES—FATHER

JIMI PHILLIP JACOBS—SON

JIMI . . .

Son . . .

son . . .

run

I start to run.

Flying out the front door

and out onto the driveway.

His name on the page blowing in the wind.

Holding it tight, but wanting to let it fly.

Just let it go.

Let it all go . . .

196

I run until I can't run anymore.
Until my legs ache
and the cold sweat starts to soak my big 'fro.
I run past the ball diamond
and out into the country.
Out onto Lilac Lane,
I run all the way to that farm
with the strange name.
Mildew or Kilgrew or somethin'.
I run past the cornfields
toward the sound of barking dogs
and the smell of country cooking.
Chimney smoke dancing over my head—
families burning first fires of the season.
Families.
I wish I could just knock on a door and
change families—
change lives—
change everything.

I wish . . .

lying in bed waiting for sleep . . .
The rain sounds like cats walking on the roof.

Now running, their paws scratching,

trying to get in.

Cold rain soaking the roof.

Inside I feel cold, too.

Inside I feel numb, from everything.

Everything that happened,

everything that is still happening.

My head feels like it's going to pop;

this dark cloud that never stops following me.

Not just Dad dying.

No. That wasn't enough.

Now, this new hell

that makes Mom's face all twisted.

Makes her back hurt,

makes her bent over

like she wasn't before.

Inside I try to find something to grab on to,

I try to hear a song, but there is none.

No song, no sound.

Nothing.

Yesterday changed everything—again.

Wiped away my hope.

All the good times with V, gone

without a trace.

Today, Mom called Dad

a master of deception.

"It all makes sense," Mom said.

"All those business trips.

So much time away from home.

Always on the road before you were born."

Mom called Dad a horrible man.

I said, "He's dead, how can you say that?"

"Tell me it's not horrible to leave your mistress

and bastard son a one hundred thousand dollar

life insurance policy and leave me and you nothing.

Tell me that's not horrible. I bet Berny didn't tell you

that, huh?

Didn't tell you that about her *wonderful* brother."

Mom's face filled with so much hate,

she didn't even look like Mom.

Her face, not Mom anymore.

Her face replaced with pain and torture and horror.

I didn't answer,
just stared into space,
stared at Mom's strange face—
looking so much older,
like she aged years overnight.

Lying in bed, waiting for sleep.
I close my eyes and wish it all away.
Everything, from that night he was shot.
To yesterday,
when Dad died
again.
All I can do is pull the covers up
and listen to the scratching paws
running fast across the roof.

CHAPTER 10

four months

A broom is drearily sweeping
Up the broken pieces of yesterday's life
Somewhere a queen is weeping
Somewhere a king has no wife

Tomorrow will be four months.
and I don't know which way is up
which way is down.
What is right
what is wrong.
Dad's been gone four months.
Not gone—dead.
Now Dad's dead again.
Sounds like a bad horror movie.
I wish it was.
Jimi sings
and I cry.
Everything is different now.
Even Hendrix songs don't sound the same,
all because of that name.
His voice reminding me of the pain.

Reminding me of

death and cheating.

Lying and

stealing.

And now there's a new "Jimi" in my life.

Not Hendrix, but this new brother

who just landed in my world.

Crashed

through the gates of my life just in time

to make everything horrible again.

Just in time to kill off what was left of my mom

and our

life.

I'm sure Mom will just let the day pass.

She can barely say his name.

She can barely say the name of my dad.

How bad is that?

Doesn't she know how terrible that makes me feel?

How it makes me sick to my stomach—to my life.

Maybe she doesn't know

doesn't care.

Doesn't matter, anyway.

Doesn't change the facts.

The facts, shredding up my insides

one day at a time.

One minute at a time.

One second at a time.

Mom.

She wakes up

with so much hate on her face.

Hate for Dad and *that woman*

and *Jimi.*

There's nothing she can do.

The money is gone.

Our money.

Even the money from Dad's secret bank account.

Gone.

Every last cent was spent

on that woman and Jimi.

Every

last

cent.

mom's words hurt

not just me, but Aunt Berny.

Aunt Berny wants to do something

for the day. The four-month anniversary.

But Mom won't hear of it.

She calls Dad a monster.

A disgrace.

She says he deserved to die.

I have to put my hands over my ears

and leave the room.

Mom yells and screams.

I think she's losing it.

Or lost it already.

Aunt Berny tells me she doesn't really mean it.

Aunt Berny tries to be supportive.

Tries not to show how Mom's words sting her.

"He was my brother. . . . He was my brother. . . ."

Aunt Berny repeats it over and over again,

like that's gonna make Mom stop her crazy talk.

Mom keeps on.

Talking about Dad like he was a stranger.

Worse than a stranger.

A criminal.

Guilty.

Maybe he is guilty, but my jury's still out.

I don't know what to believe.

Don't know what I *want* to believe.

Mom's words stabbing me.

Mom's words

hurt. . . .

anniversary

Tears and silence and

there's nothing I can do.

Can't bring him back.

Can't change the past.

I let the day go

hope it goes fast.

Try to keep busy and not think about it.

Try to keep busy and

wait for tomorrow to come.

Tomorrow will be better.

Tomorrow will be just another day.

two worlds

"I know yesterday was hard. Are you okay?

You don't seem okay. Do you want to talk about it?

It might get harder with Thanksgiving coming up.

You know you can talk to me if you

want. Anytime. It's cool, okay?"

"Thanks, I know."

V being V. Being there for me, being my "friend."

She knows yesterday was

the four-month anniversary.

She knows just enough.

Just what I want her to know.

Which isn't that much.

Because, I still don't know if I can trust her.

I still don't know . . .

"Last night I got into another fight with my dad.

I hate him sometimes. He just doesn't get me.

Doesn't get that I'm different than him.

I don't want to be like him. What's wrong

with the music I like and the shows I watch?

I'll never be like him.

All closed-minded and you know . . ."

"Prejudiced?" I finish V's sentence.

She just nods. Not even wanting to say the word.

Seems like V has two worlds she lives in.

Her school world with me

open and free.

And then her home world.

Her dad, who tries to run her

tell her what to do

what to think

what to be.

Maybe V hangs out with me

just to get back at her dad.

Maybe she's just trying to make him mad.

Tells him she likes this little biracial kid

with the big 'fro

and the weird clothes.

What do you think about that, Dad?

just friends

"I'm so glad we're friends."

That's it. The kiss of death.

The five words no guy wants to hear.

Final confirmation of my worst fear.

Breaking the news to me like

I should have known it all along.

Like I should have known we were "just friends."

I feel so dumb for thinking it was something more.

For wishing it was something more.

Maybe her dad stopped it

from being something more.

Standing in the lunch line,

I grab my burger and fries.

Wanting to scream at her.

But I still like her.

I still need her. . . .

I *want* to tell V about my dad.

About this "other woman" and my half brother.

But I can't. If I tell her then it makes it real.

Even though we are friends.

That's what friends are for, right?

Wrong.

Being friends with V is not a good thing.

I want more. . . .

Doesn't help me out at all, not in this school.

Goodwill points for having a dead dad,

erased

when your best friend is blond and fine and—

you are not.

Like right now, in the lunch line

I can feel it.

Kids think we are *together*,

So more hate gets thrown my way.

Mean looks and sometimes worse.

I pretend I don't hear what they say.

Calling us *Midnight and Daylight/Salt and Pepper*

and other ignorant stuff.

V says to just ignore it.

But I know it bothers her too.

Her friends don't talk to her as much

as they used to. . . .

Her friends don't like me at all.

I wish we were *together*.

Maybe one day

we will be . . .

but

for now

"just friends."
I hate
"just friends."
I am always
"just friends."

night song
Late at night
in my room . . .
words bleed onto paper.
The truth appearing before my eyes.
I grab my guitar . . .
can't keep everything inside. . . .
Days
go into
nights
go into
days
way too much time in this stupid place.
My: how can you call this a life?
SUCKS.
Never know who you can trust;

The Truth is just too much.

Everything ending

in Death

and pain.

Everything ending

again . . .

Too many days/too many nights/

Never enough time.

can't even look at the name

The name I used to love.

The name I used to write all over my notebooks.

The name I used to write *everywhere.*

Now it's not the same.

Those four letters look different now.

When I see Jimi—I see *him.*

Now just a four letter word

who stole *my* name/who stole everything.

A brother I didn't know I had.

Even if he is just a half, he's taken so much.

So much from me and Mom.

Hate rises

into my head and my chest.

My fists are clenched a lot now.

I want to hit.

And hurt.

I want to make myself feel better.

But I don't know how. . . .

Can't even look at that name.

Now my Hendrix Poster doesn't look the same.

Hard to turn on my DigiTunes,

all because

of

him.

He's ruining everything.

Jimi's killing Jimi—

Hendrix

The last thing I had.

That reminded me of Dad.

He's taking it all away. . . .

at school

At my locker

in the halls.

Everywhere.

Bobby Powers stares.

He tries to scare me with a look.

Hasn't said a word since that day.

That day he said so much.

But now he just stares.

He thinks he's got me.

He thinks I'm just a punk.

I'm starting to hide,

making myself even smaller than I am.

Hiding inside myself.

V can tell something's wrong.

I still haven't told her about my dad,

but I told her about Bobby.

Not everything.

Not exactly what he said.

Didn't tell her I just froze.

Kept my mouth shut.

He thinks he's got me.

He thinks I'm just a punk.
Bobby Powers stares,
but I
just
look away.

sometimes
I get so lonely.
It makes my skin cold.
Gives me chills, but not the good kind.
I know I could at least *try* to make friends,
but I don't want to.
Definitely not in this school.
I'm on the outside and getting farther away
every day.
If everything is true about
Dad
then what's the use?
Now the cold gets colder
and my face starts to buzz.
I'm walking home from school
but I don't go home.

I take a detour
and walk through lawns and
backyards,
weaving my way
to anyplace
to nowhere.
Not caring where
I end up.
Not caring at all.
I don't even want to see tomorrow.
Don't even want to finish today.
Sometimes it gets so bad that—
but I would never do it.
I couldn't leave Mom and Aunt Berny.
I couldn't do that to them.
I just couldn't . . .

"how can we have thanksgiving?"
In the middle of talking with Aunt Berny
and I can't hold it back.
Cutting me like a piece of broken glass.
Snuck up on me this time.

Maybe I didn't want it to come.

But now it's here.

Now, in two days

the first real

holiday.

Holidays are the worst after a death.

That's what everybody says.

Every day's the worst,

if you ask me.

I don't want turkey,

I don't want stuffing.

I don't want Thanksgiving this year.

Aunt Berny sitting in her Berny Chair.

A green rocker that's seen better days.

Mom in the kitchen clanging pots and pans.

Getting her anger out. But not doing much cooking.

Aunt Berny's eyes start to close

rocking herself to sleep.

I click on the TV.

Changing channels as fast as I can.

Nothing on.

Mom comes in and sits next to me on the couch.

"How can we have Thanksgiving without Dad?"

I hear myself sound so young.

A little kid crying for his dad.

Mom tries to smile, but I can tell it's hard.

She flinches when I say "Dad."

Like it sends a shock through her body.

She doesn't say a word.

She doesn't even touch me.

Doesn't even hold my hand

or rub my back.

Maybe she blames me.

Maybe I remind her of Dad.

I start clicking again.

Distracting myself.

Mom pretends to watch TV with me.

But I know I'm watching by myself.

She's left me alone

again.

the pain remains the same

Homework after dinner.

Studying for my test.

I can feel the stress seeping through the walls.

Coming through my door.

The storm after the calm.

Pulling me downstairs.

Pulling me down.

Papers and bank statements piled high

on the coffee table,

more pain spilling onto the floor.

Mom going over it again.

Going over all the stuff from that

safety-deposit box.

Every few days she does this.

But it always comes out the same.

Nothing changes.

Every time,

the pain remains the same. . . .

"Thousands of dollars, Berny.

Thousands and thousands of dollars to that—

that woman

and her son.

Probably hush money to keep them quiet.

Look at this address,

some post office box I never

even knew about.

Getting his mail from his other life.

Hiding it from me.

Hiding everything from me.

I should have paid more attention.

Should have known what was going on.

He always said everything was taken care of.

He took care of me, alright,

took care of me *real* good. . . ."

poison

"All those good years he was raking in the cash.

Those publishing deals and ASCAP royalties,

I thought he was putting some away.

Saving it for us. For me and Keith.

Saving for our future.

He said he was putting away 'big chunks.'

He was putting it away alright;

for that bitch and his bastard son.

Look at this, Berny.

Here's a statement from eight years ago, here's one

from last year.

Who knows how long he's been doing this.

All those years

all that money.

The last few years he gave them even more.

A whole lot more.

When we had less, they got more.

What kind of animal was he?

He lied about everything.

His business was in the toilet, Berny.

He lost his publishing deal three years ago and never

even told me.

He had nothin' comin' in.

Nothin'.

And everything he had is gone.

GONE!"

Now Mom is yelling,

yelling loud at the top of her lungs.

Aunt Berny telling her to calm,

just calm down. Aunt Berny looking

tired and sad—confused like she can't

believe what her brother did.

Looking stunned like she didn't know who

her brother was; but still not believing this is true.

"This has to be a mistake,

some kind of terrible mistake."

Aunt Berny saying the same thing she always says.

Shaking her head and waving her hands

like she's trying to make all the papers disappear.

"These statements don't lie, Berny.

They just don't lie."

Dad was transferring our life a little at a time.

More and more with every passing year.

Mom didn't notice.

Dad would replace just enough to make it okay.

Problem was, it was never enough.

After he lost his publishing deal

he started taking from my trust/my future.

Took from anywhere he could.

No matter how bad he was doing,

he had money for *them*.

Lots of money.

Even when *we* were struggling.

They were taken care of.

He always took care of *them*.

"Unpaid loans—second and third mortgages."

Mom is spitting out the words like poison.

Poison that's seeping into my body,

making me sick.

Making me wish this wasn't real.

I start to lose my breath.

I close my eyes and try to see Dad.

His face.

Anything.

But I can't see him.

He's fading away.

All this poison is killing him

again.

I go back upstairs and take my pill.

Closing my eyes

looking for Dad.

I listen to Jimi

but it's so hard now.

It's so hard. . . .

Somewhere a queen is weeping

Somewhere a king has no wife

CHAPTER 11

no thanks

Mom moves slow in the kitchen.

Night before Thanksgiving.

It seems so hard for her to move,

like she's fighting some force only she can see.

Fighting Dad.

Mom

not even working part-time anymore.

Quit her job at the craft store.

"She just can't handle much now," Aunt Berny says.

Concern and worry changing the sound of her voice.

Like there's something stuck in her throat.

Aunt Berny makes all the food. Mom just

pretends to help.

Aunt Berny doing everything now.

Mom so depressed all the time.

Permanent lines and sadness on her face—

that never go away.

Thanksgiving, yeah right.

I don't want to thank anybody,

and I don't feel like giving.

So why don't they just cancel it this year.

Why don't they just cancel the
whole
stupid
day.

not the same

Everything looks the same.

The food, the dishes.

Smells the same, too.

But it's definitely not the same.

Not the same at all without Dad.

Not the same knowing his past.

What he did.

How he hurt us so bad.

How he's still hurting us
every day.

Mom hardly touches her food.

Aunt Berny is eating everything in sight.

Nothing touches her appetite.

I just sit and hope the day goes fast.

Just get through dinner, get through dessert.

Then it will be over.

Dumb holiday—just an excuse to eat tons of food.

Everything looks the same.

Smells the same, too.

But

it's definitely not

the same.

Not the same at all.

black stone

I go to my room.

Thanksgiving football is on.

But I can't watch.

Reminds me too much of last year.

Me and Dad watching the game.

Laughing at the commercials.

Laughing at everything.

I shut my eyes and see that black stone rise.

Rising up from behind the trees.

Now Dad's got front-row seats.

Front row for that stupid cemetery road.

Cars and hearses passing by—

souls on their way to their final resting place.

Not a good seat, if you ask me.

Front row or not.

I see that black stone a lot now.

When I close my eyes, when I open them, too.

I hate that black stone.

I hate it so much.

But I wish I could touch it.

Feel his name against my fingertips—

cold and smooth.

His name is all I have.

And memories of

MAJ.

The guy who used to be my dad.

Memories fading fast,

trying to hold on to the good

when all around is bad.

I try to shake away the black stone from my mind.

But I can't.

I can hear Aunt Berny screaming at the TV.

Yelling at the game.

I cover my ears.

I cover my face.

But I just can't escape
that black stone.

saturday-morning cereal

I take another spoonful and hate him some more.
I wonder what he's like,
this half brother who's ruining our lives.
My dad's *other* "project."
The one he was working on since
before I was born.
Jimi's three years older than me.
Sixteen.
I wonder what he's like?
I hope he doesn't have any friends.
I hope he's stuck on the outside too.
I hope he has a harder time than I do.
I hope his life is hell and hurt and it's
only getting worse.
I wonder what he's like,
but
I don't really care.

thanksgiving break

going fast.

Like Mom.

Into the black.

Into the background.

My hate getting stronger and stronger.

Can't keep holding it in.

I look at Mom—(just a shell

of what she used to be . . .)

and all I see

is Dad.

Not the man I knew.

But the thief—the cheat that used

my mom

and me.

Abused our trust,

abused us.

I see him beating her

with his past every day.

Making her weaker.

Dad and that woman—Denise

and

his son.

Jimi.

He's really to blame.

He's the evidence.

The bastard son

like Mom says.

He's the bribe.

The piggy bank who needs to cry.

Like Mom.

Like me.

My hate getting stronger,

making me want to do something.

I should get that money back.

Steal it back from Jimi.

From Denise.

Rob *them* like

they robbed me.

Mom is too weak, too weak to even try.

Aunt Berny just works all the time.

Nobody is standing up for us.

For our life.

Nobody wants to fight.

Anger rises to the top
like curdled cream
ready to make you sick.
But I'm tired of being the one that's sick.
I'm tired of being the one that hurts.
I'm tired.

hi

After the break
Monday morning
I pass V in the hallway.
She smiles and says hi.
I say hi, too.
She says she'll see me at lunch.
I say okay.
Seems like me and V are getting
further away
from each other.
Maybe it was just the break.
Don't really talk on the phone.
We really just talk at school.
That one date was it.

I guess.

Maybe her dad, shutting us down.

He's probably too strong.

Has her back under his thumb.

I want to tell V about Denise and Jimi.

That I have to do something to make things right.

To try to get our life back.

I feel the words ready to come.

I feel the words on the tip of my tongue—

but V turns and walks away.

I watch her walk down the hall.

Her jeans teasing me some more.

I watch V catching up to Mona and Patti.

I watch V

leaving me

behind.

the return of bobby powers
(bobby's back)
"Where you think you're going, hippie freak?"
Big arms and dripping sweat,
no neck all up in my face.

Bobby takes me by surprise.

I hold my ground, at least for now,

but I feel my foundation cracking.

Slowly backing up, looking for a way out.

Another way out of the lunchroom.

"Where you goin' *brutha*?

Who said you were allowed to leave?"

Coles is behind me, pushing me with his shoulder.

He's like a carbon copy of Bobby.

His right-hand man.

Both of them grown from birth

specifically to be big and mean

and

ready to kick my ass.

Big bellies surrounded by muscle—

no-necks closing in on me fast.

I freeze. I can't speak,

but I know

this is my chance.

I have to stand up for myself now.

I have to stand up to these

ignorant-dumb-racist-red-no-necks.

There's no one left.

No Dad,

or Mom.

No Aunt Berny

to calm them down.

Nobody's left.

I'm the last one.

Dad always told me to stand up for myself.

But how can I believe what came out of his mouth?

Dad is a lie.

Just like his life.

I am standing, but I'm still too small.

Even smaller now.

Smaller by the second.

But I know

there's nobody left.

Nobody left

but

me.

"back up off me."

Four words coming from someone else.

Couldn't be me.

I still feel small,

but something just got tall.

Inside—feeling just a little strong.

"Back up off me, you stupid, ignorant rednecks."

Four words turn into eight.

I just can't take it anymore.

Always afraid.

Of everything

and

everyone.

Inside—getting just a little strong.

They'll probably kill me now.

They probably will.

Still . . .

Those words came from:

somewhere

came from:

someone

came from:

me.

the hawk

Waiting to feel the punch I know will come.

Waiting for the pain.

Waiting.

But it doesn't come.

Saved by Ms. Digby "The Hawk."

"Let's break it up."

She stops it before it starts.

Ms. Digby watches everything and everyone.

Must have seen it all go down.

I walk out of the caf, and never look back.

Good thing for Bobby "The Hawk" was out.

I smile to myself,

knowing that's not the truth.

Knowing that the Hawk swooped down and saved

my black-and-white ass from certain doom.

Problem is,

Bobby knows it too.

CHAPTER 12

out of the blue

Sitting in the library at school.

Looking up dead presidents.

Not the kind I need—not the kind I can spend.

When out of the blue

V pops in and invites me to Christmas Eve

at her house.

From nothin' to somethin'

in seconds flat.

Maybe it's a trap.

Maybe her dad's gonna kill me

when I come over.

Okay, now that's crazy.

Crazy, but anything's possible these days.

Sitting in the library.

V is as casual as can be.

Like it's just an ordinary thing.

Two weeks until it might be the

end of me.

Or the beginning.

Man, I'll never figure women out.

I know she saw my mouth drop.

Picking it up slowly off the floor,
I think I said Yes, I'll be there.
I think I did.
But
my mouth *was* on the floor. . . .

"watch your back"
The words whispered in my ears.
Like something romantic.
Except this is a warning.
From one of Bobby's thugs.
Have to look over my shoulder
for just one more week,
then it's Christmas break.
But I'm not scared.
Been through too much to be scared.
If I get my butt kicked, then
so be it.
But I'm not goin' down
without a fight.
"Watch your back,"
another kid whispers to me.

"You watch yours,"
I say to him.
"You watch yours . . ."

so bad, so fast
I can hear Aunt Berny on the phone,
she's got her quiet-don't-want-anybody-to-hear-me-
talking-on-the-phone-voice on.
But
I can hear. I can hear loud and clear.
Upstairs after school, my newfound strength
slipping away.
Hearing too much again.
Hearing enough.
"So many bills," she says.
Aunt Berny sounds nervous.
Talking to a friend, someone she can confide in.
Now with her quiet voice on,
the words come pouring out:
"He's having a hard time of it."
"I don't know if she'll ever be the same."
"I don't know how long I can keep this up,

I just don't know . . ."
My stomach jumps upside down.
I take a deep breath.
What if Aunt Berny can't make the rent?
What if she has to move and kicks us out?
What if me and Mom have to go live on the streets?
How would we survive?
How could Dad do this to us?
How could things get so bad
so fast?

stepping on the past
I look in my closet and see the past
hanging on hangers.
All my psychedelic clothes
stuff from Dad's treasure chest.
I should just burn it.
Don't even want to *give it away*.
It should be destroyed,
like what Dad's doing to us.
From the grave—giving us pain and hurt,
taking our love,

making us hate.

I grab a handful of clothes

and throw them on the floor.

Stepping on them, grinding my sneakers into the

fabric of the shirts.

Stepping on the past, stepping on Dad.

It makes me feel better, like I'm getting back at him.

My few minutes of revenge . . .

my few minutes—

Then,

I kneel on the floor and pick up the clothes.

I know I can't burn them, I can't throw them away.

As much as I want to; I can't.

It's all I have left of Dad.

It's all I have.

life

Nowhere to turn

nowhere to hide.

Nothing works

nothing seems right.

I try every playlist, every group on my DigiTunes.

Can't find a song

I can lose myself in.

Can't find a band

that knows what I'm going through.

What I'm feeling.

What my world

has become.

Life ain't no love song. . . .

i tell V everything

One day before Christmas break

I tell V everything.

Hard to say the words at first.

Makes it more real, too real.

I tell her about Dad;

how he died—twice.

I tell her about Denise and Jimi,

and all the lies and stealing:

The safety-deposit box

and how Mom is lost

and may never be found.

V listens to every word;
never interrupts, just lets
me talk.
All the way through to the end.
Finally, she nods and gives me
a soft smile.
"You'll be okay, you're strong," she says.
"You'll get through this, you will."
Talking outside, after school.
I want to ask V why she invited me for
Christmas Eve.
But I don't. Maybe I don't wanna know?
Sitting on the grassy knoll next to the band room.
The grassy knoll, where couples hang out.
Both of us silent, for a while.
Listening to
the end-of-the-day sounds—kids and buses,
laughs and shouts.
Feels a lot colder now.
"I have to find him," I tell V.
My voice still trying to convince me.
I'm going to find this kid. This kid with my name.

This kid with my blood flowin' through his veins.

Eating up *our* food. Spendin' all *our* money.

This kid

who my dad loved more

than me.

This kid who got

everything.

This half brother.

He's gonna know what he did.

How he hurt me and Mom and Aunt Berny.

He's going to pay for this.

One way

or

another . . .

he's going to pay.

"I have to find him, V.

I have to."

having fun

Snow falling fast.

Thick flakes sticking in my hair.

Sticking on the driveway.

First snow falling on the first day of Christmas break.

Me and Aunt Berny having a snowball fight.

I don't tell her that I'm gonna find Jimi.

She doesn't need the worry

she doesn't need to know.

Snow falling harder now.

Aunt Berny throwing harder, too.

The wind blows the snow across my boots

as I try to duck out of the way.

Snowball smacks me in the face.

We both laugh hard/for the first time in ages.

Not thinking about a thing.

Just

having

fun. . . .

must be hard

After the snowball fight,

Aunt Berny's got that far-off look in her eyes.

The one she gets when I know
she's thinkin' about Dad.
The one she gets when I know she's gone back
to the past.
Her past,
growin' up with Dad.
"I remember—when—"
she starts to tell a story, but stops herself fast.
Must be hard.
She's caught in the middle.
Like me and Mom
but even worse.
Must be hard for her to choose a side.
She lost a brother. But I know she blames him, too.
For what he's done.
For what he didn't do to take care of
me and Mom.
Must be hard to keep her mouth shut
when Mom goes on with her crazy talk.
Saying she's glad my dad is dead.
It's hard for me.
Must be hard for her. . . .

Aunt Berny kisses me good-bye,

and goes to work.

I finish my hot chocolate, slurping the last drop.

I stare into the bottom of the cup,

wishing that every day could be like this.

Snowball fights and

hot chocolate

and

nothing

else. . . .

later on that day . . .

Mom standing at the kitchen sink.

Bathrobe and slippers,

her hair uncombed.

The way she looks

pushing me more

to move

on what I have to do.

To find Jimi.

To find his mom.

To find out more.

After I kick his ass

I'm gonna interrogate him.

Like in the movies.

Find out what he knows.

Find out everything.

Good, bad, or ugly,

I have to know what he knows.

He's got my money.

He's got my name.

I have to find out why.

Why he got everything

and I got nothing.

Why Dad loved him more.

Dad is dead.

But Jimi's alive.

I'll squeeze him till he screams.

I'll squeeze him till he tells me

everything.

Jimi's gonna talk.

If he knows what's good for

him, he will.

2 plus 2

Mom knows more

than she wants to.

Mom putting 2 and 2 together standing at the

kitchen sink.

Trying to get a drink of water.

Her hands shaking.

She's in real bad shape.

Hard for me to even look at her.

But I have a job to do.

Try to get Mom to talk.

Help me figure out where to start.

Where to look for Jimi.

Johnnie Cochran James/asking leading questions.

Don't want her to know what I'm up to.

Mom talking quiet and slow,

telling me about all of Dad's trips

before I was born. Dad had lots of work.

Lots of work in Ohio.

Dad taking extended stays.

Mom thought he was visiting Aunt Berny.

Mom thought.

Always going to Ohio. For years.

Dad had an artist up in Cleveland.

A great new singer . . .

"I was such a fool. I should've known.

How could I have been so blind?"

Mom closes her eyes, now bent over at the sink,

taking a drink of water.

I turn to leave, but I can't look back.

Can't look at Mom,

dying a slow death,

one day at a time.

Just a fragment of what she used to be.

All because of Dad and Denise.

All because of

Jimi.

i get to work

going through all that safety-deposit stuff.

Mom leaves it out all the time now.

Like some kind of war memorial.

But the war isn't over yet.

I'm looking for an address.

A phone number.

Anything that I can use to make contact.

Anything I can use to find them.

I wish Mom hadn't sold Dad's computer.

Probably a treasure chest of clues.

Mom didn't have a clue when she sold it.

She just didn't know—*There's a bank stamp.*

First—Fifth Bank,

Cleveland, Ohio—like that birth certificate said.

Cleveland, like what Mom said, too.

It's a start,

but it's not enough.

CHAPTER **13**

christmas eve
at the Sweets'
Long table and lots of food.

White shirt, black pants is who I am for this
Christmas Eve.

Not my choice—Aunt Berny blocked the door.

Wouldn't let me out in my '60s clothes.

No talking at the table.

The opposite of how it is—

how it *was* at our house.

Mr. Sweet stares through his mashed potatoes
and doesn't smile.

I can tell he's uncomfortable.

Not really looking at me, just politely ignoring.

Both of us just trying to get through the meal.

Mrs. Sweet holds court with her best friend,

just in from Texas. V's older sister, Kate,

is at *her* best friend's house. She won't be in
until tomorrow.

"Why am I here?"

I whisper to V in between bites of too-dry turkey
and even drier stuffing.

"Because I like you and you're my friend,"
V whispers back. Smiling a smile that
melts me completely. Warming my soul
making me feel almost whole,
just for a second.
Then I come back to the tension and stress
of this *all* White Christmas
Eve.
I feel like the Sweets are really sour.
Just tolerating me for the evening.
Just tolerating the brown shortie with the big 'fro,
just tolerating me long enough
until it's time to go. . . .
Me and V sit together on the couch and watch
It's a Wonderful Life.
A wonderful life,

yeah, right.

christmas day
(a gift from the past)
Presents in the morning

dessert at night.

In between I am busy.

In my head,

trying to find Jimi.

Keeps my mind off the day.

What it means.

What it used to mean.

I want him to feel what I feel.

Pain.

What I carry around every day.

My heart getting caught in a car door.

Slammed shut

all ripped up

and I can't

get it free.

He needs to feel

just like me.

I keep searching those papers.

Over and over again.

But all I have is Cleveland.

Then I see it. Just a piece of paper

folded twice

and tucked inside a plain white envelope.

Something I didn't see before.

Lost in all this painful past.

The paper sticking its head out.

Trying to tell me something.

I pick it up and unfold it.

Just a few words.

But it's all I need.

From: Dsong1@jackflash.com
To: Majicman55@firemail.com
Subject: (none)

Thanks a lot. It came just in time. But please don't write
me or Jimi. It's just too much for us. It's just too much.

D.

getting closer

A piece of the past

A piece of Dad.

Don't know what it means

don't need to.

All I need is what I have.

266

An e-mail address.

Hot on the trail.

Getting closer.

the two musketeers

Behind the stacks in the Hollow Falls Public Library.

Me and V hot on the trail of a couple of thieves.

Using a public computer to cover our tracks.

Don't want to get Aunt Berny involved.

Just in case things get out of hand.

We have a plan. But we have to work fast.

Only have a small window of opportunity.

V helps me with the e-mail.

Helps me set our trap . . .

From: lc13@firemail.com
To: Dsong1@jackflash.com
Subject: Emergency

Dear Denise,
My name is Keith James. Marvin (Anthony) James's
"other" son. I really need to talk to you and your son Jimi,
face-to-face. I will be in Cleveland over New Year's.
I hope you will find it in your heart to see me. It has
been very hard since my dad was killed. We've lost our

house, our money, our life. We are struggling in every way.
My mother is getting worse every day. Too many questions
left unanswered. I really hope you can help.
I really hope you'll see me.

Sincerely,
Keith James

"You catch more flies with honey than you do with
vinegar."
V looks proud.
Looking over her handy work,
I wanted to make it more harsh,
but V said no.
"This way you draw her in.
Give her a false sense of security.
Then, when she least expects it . . .
ATTACK."

no reply

Checking for days, and time running out.
Only one week left of break.
Me and V checking every day—
all the time—

running out.
Still
no reply.

not a hero now
In my room.
Waiting for an answer from
Jimi's mom.
Dad's song comes into my head.
I pick up my guitar, but something's changed.
Shooting down to my fingers—touching the strings.
Something's changed.
Dad's not the same.
He's not a hero now.
"He's a thief." Mom's words so hard to believe.
Until I hear my own
until I hear my song:

> *He's a thief*
> *A lie*
> *A cheat*
> *A thief*
> *A lie*

A cheat
Never was what I thought he was
Never was what I thought he was
Never was
My
Hero dad

My guitar falls from my hands,
neck hits the floor
strings about to break.

Tears in my eyes.

time is running out
Only two days 'til New Year's Eve.
Still haven't heard a thing.
Maybe she won't write back.
Maybe she doesn't care.
Maybe I'll never know
anything more.

contact

From: Dsong1@jackflash.com
To: lc13@firemail.com
Subject: Re: Emergency

Dear Keith,
My mom won't see you, but I will. Meet me at the Rock n Roll Hall of Fame, Cleveland, New Year's Day. 1 pm at the information desk. Just ask for me, they know me there.

Jimi

e-mail in my head

Dear Jimi,
Got ya.

taking the pictures down
Have to make right
what Dad made wrong.
Tomorrow I'm going to Cleveland
only got one shot.

Has to be tomorrow.

But

tonight—one by one—

I'm taking them down.

When I see his face all I can think about is Mom.

Pictures from a past I don't want to know anymore.

Dad and his lies, his secret life.

With Denise and Jimi.

How could he look Mom in the eye?

How could he act like everything was fine?

Like everything was normal.

How could he do it?

One by one, I'm taking them down.

Have to make right

what Dad made wrong.

"have fun"

is all Aunt Berny says.

Mom just stands there.

Looking through me.

Told them I was going with V's family

up to Lake Erie

for New Year's Eve.

Well, it's not all a lie.

Me and V's plan workin' like a charm.

Aunt Berny called V's mom.

Or she thought she did.

Really, it was V's older sister, Kate.

Aunt Berny bought it.

I think she's too stressed and busy

to even worry.

Just as long as I

come back. . . .

I guess they're glad I'm going.

One less person to worry about.

I probably just make it harder.

Harder for them, when I'm here.

Almost six months since the murder,

and now it's time

for my revenge.

Not against the killer.

But the real assassin.

Now it's time for Jimi to face the music.

To face me.

Outside is freezing cold.
But I don't feel it.
Walking to the street
I hear a song pass by;
I grab it
and keep warm,
singing this song
out into the quiet cold:

Face the music
Face the past
Time to face my "other"
Half
brother
You can't run
You can't hide
I've got you in my sights
I'll see you soon
My
Brother

I'll see you soon . . .

CHAPTER 14

on the road

with

V and her older sister, Kate.

She's on break from college.

V's parents said it was cool.

They don't know *I'm* going, too. . . .

Kate's real cool for doin' what she did.

Her and V are tight, as tight as sisters can get.

Climbing into Kate's cool Silver Flash.

One of those cool new SUVs.

Kate said she'd drive us up to Cleveland/ she's got

friends she wants to see.

Gonna go to a party on New Year's Eve.

Me and V will stay in/at the motel.

She booked separate rooms, of course.

I hate *of course.* . . .

backseat

Alone in the backseat

three-hour trip.

V up front with Kate, talkin' a mile a minute.

V in her hot purple sweater.

Just when I thought I was cool with

"Just friends,"

I get that feeling again.

I try to push it away . . .

watching the cars pass us by.

Watching the big eighteen-wheelers choke up the

road.

Watching V in that incredible purple sweater. . . .

rest stop

But I'm not tired.

We gas up and

get fast food.

My usual burger and fries.

"What are you gonna say when you see him?"

Kate asks, shoving fries into her mouth.

"I don't know the exact words,

but when the time comes

I know it will flow. I just know."

I don't want to say any more.

I make it sound like I'm just gonna talk,

but that's only the first part.
If he isn't smart he's gonna get a whole lotta hurt
crashin' down on him.
I don't care if he's older
or
bigger
or
stronger.
I will do whatever I have
to do.
Whatever
it takes.

longer than i think

Three hours is more like four.
With all the New Year's traffic.
Even in Ohio there's a lot of cars.
I try to keep my mind off V's purple sweater.
Try to keep my mind off what's *underneath* her
sweater.
But that's close to impossible.
I think about what I have to do.

I get ready for Jimi.

Getting strong in my mind.

I have to get back our life

For Mom.

For Aunt Berny.

For

me.

creepy

"We're here. This is your stop," Kate says.

She drops us off.

She's staying with her friends.

So it's just me and V staying at this prison.

That's what it looks like/from the outside.

Columns and a high wall.

Must be the *Hotel California*.

CREEPY is what I think.

Chipped gray paint and a very unwelcome sign that

says:

THE LANCAZAR *est. 1868.*

Place is huge, too.

Takes up more than a block/easy.

Scary lookin'. Probably haunted.

I don't even want to go in.

Maybe I'll just sleep outside.

Probably safer.

the room
(so nasty)

The room smells bad.

Like real old Chinese food that's been left out

for a month.

Worse than that.

I sit down on the bed,

checking it first to make sure it's clean.

Barely.

This place is so nasty.

V apologizes.

She said she thought it would be

a cool place to stay.

Something different.

"Definitely doesn't look like it does on the Internet."

V puts a towel down on the chair before she sits.

historical landmark or not,

it's a dump.

"It's gonna be one long, nasty night."

V smiles, but neither of us are laughing.

new year's eve on TV

We watch the flavor-of-the-month bands

play their hits

and

I get homesick for New York.

Watching all the people in Times Square.

I was there.

Once.

With Dad. It was so sweet.

We got to see The Strangers

a cool band that Dad knew.

Got backstage and everything.

Hard to think about that night,

knowing now that Dad was living a lie.

Living a secret life.

I know that now

but

then

he was just Dad standing in Times Square

holding on to his son . . .

watching the ball drop on

New Year's Eve.

V kisses me on the cheek/brings me back

from Dad and Times Square.

V kisses me on the cheek and says,

"Happy New Year."

"Happy New Year," I say back.

Still not believing she kissed me.

Still not believing it's a new year.

Still,

not believing . . .

new year's day

A new day

A new year.

I feel the same,

but maybe after today

things will change

maybe after today . . .

If you drive into Lake Erie you've gone too far . . .

That's what the directions say.

Kate's gonna drop us off,

pick us up later.

Don't know how long I'll need.

Maybe five minutes

maybe all day.

I just don't know.

"I'll be right next to you the whole time," V says,

smiling her *sweet* smile

that could melt the polar ice caps.

"Thanks, but this is something I'm gonna have to do

alone.

This has to be just Jimi and me,

just

Jimi and Me. . . ."

heaven

The Rock and Roll Hall of Fame.

I see it first.

Dad talked about taking me here
but he never did. *I wonder why.*
It's like a building coming down from
rock 'n' roll heaven.
The final resting place for the true immortals.
Everybody's there.
Sitting right against the water.
The shore of Lake Erie.
Coolest building I've ever seen.
Way cool and modern.
Like some futuristic spaceship right on the water.
For a minute I forget about
my half brother the thief . . .
and the money . . .
and the real reason I'm here.
Right now: I am at the pearly gates
of rock 'n' roll heaven.
Getting ready to see my *real* heroes.
The ones I've only seen in movies.
The ones I've only heard on CDs.
The ones I've only dreamed about. . . .

we're early

Twenty bucks a pop,

but me and V get a discount.

We use Kate's Triple A card.

We're early but it's okay.

Give me some time to see the place.

Even cooler on the inside than the outside.

An hour early but I still check the information desk.

Nobody standing around waiting,

so I ask.

They say Jimi's on lunch break.

So he works here.

Makes me even more mad.

He gets to come here every day?

And get paid?

Me and V go down to the ground level.

The only exhibit I really want to see.

Jimi Hendrix has like a whole wing.

His whole life/everything he ever did or said

or wrote.

I **am** a kid in a candy store.

He even has a theater.

The Jimi Hendrix Theater.

Gonna save that for last.

I grab V's hand and pull her past the

people at the coat check.

No time for that.

Only have an hour to get my Hendrix on.

Only have an hour . . .

ladies and gentlemen,

please welcome

the one,

the only . . .

Born Johnny Allen Hendrix

on November 27th, 1942, in Seattle, Washington.

His name was changed four years later

to James Marshall Hendrix.

Often played a re-strung right-handed guitar

throughout his career,

a '68 Fender Strat.

Wrote the song "Angel" after having

a dream about his mother.

Played acoustic Black Widow guitar
toward the end of his life.
played it on the song "Mojo Man,"
which was never released.

Originally titled, "Purple Haze, Jesus Saves,"
written backstage in a dressing room at the
Upper Cut Club in London in 1966.

So much to take in, my eyes get blurry.
The closest I'll ever come to
meeting him.
This genius who took six strings
and made sounds that no one
had ever heard before.
Or since.
Anyone who has *ever* picked up a guitar
has been influenced by him.
He changed the way the guitar was played.
His songs—his sounds had to be

from outer space.

He was *so* out of this world. . . .

I can almost feel his presence.

Looking at his handwritten lyrics—

the cool way he wrote

"purple" and "haze."

His acoustic/electric guitar

his black felt hat with the silk scarf . . .

Face-to-face with the first black rock star.

History staring me in the face.

The greatest of the great . . .

THE ONE

THE ONLY

JIMI HENDRIX

it's one-thirty already

"Now you're late, I'll just come up with you,

then I'll leave," V says,

grabbing me by the arm and pulling me onto the

escalator.

I hope he's there.

Probably chickened out.

Went home.

I know he doesn't want to face me.

My mind feels like it's still in the Hendrix theater.

Watching Jimi jam on the big screen.

On his knees lighting his axe

on

FIRE.

Playing behind his back/with his teeth.

But that was just for show.

It was his music that changed the world.

So much larger than life.

Even bigger on that screen.

My mind is still there, but

my body is riding up the escalator

on my way to come face-to-face

with the past—again.

But

this past is pain.

This past is hurt.

This past has the nerve to call himself

Jimi.

Almost to the top now . . .

I bet he chickened out

I bet he did.

face-to-face

I see him first.

That has to be him.

He's a skinny/scrawny thing.

Actually looks *younger* than me.

V is holding my hand.

Walking slow

toward the big sign that says INFORMATION/TICKETS

Getting close . . .

That face: so much like Dad.

His hair cut close to his head.

Now he sees me.

He doesn't get up.

He doesn't move.

Scared . . .

He just sits there and waits.

Me and V

pick up the pace.
Every step makes me hate him
more.
Every step makes me want to scream.
Every step brings me closer to:
that face; so much like Dad . . .

looks so much like Dad.

"you must be keith"
he says,
sitting so smug behind the desk.
I go Left.
I go South.
I go
OFF.

explosion
I am a machine gun
with unlimited clips.
My words ripping him up.

"Do you know what you've done . . .

You stupid scrawny thing . . . All the pain you've

caused . . . The money you stole.

How could you do this?

We lost our house/had to move.

My mom is gone/she's not even my mom

anymore/just barely hangin' on.

Are you happy with yourself?

Happy with the pain you've caused?

Tricked my dad into loving you more

giving you more . . .

You and your evil mom.

The truth hurts/don't it?

Look at you, you're a pathetic piece of trash.

I'm little, and I could kick your ass.

Maybe I will.

Maybe I should just jump over that desk and—"

Veronica gets in my face. Trying to stop me.

Trying, but she can't.

Nobody can.

This kid's gonna know what pain

really is.

This kid's gonna know . . .

"you're such a coward
You're probably not even worth beating up.

You're just a scared little runt.

That's what you are.

Sitting there, you won't even get up.

That's because you can't defend what you've done.

You go and run to your mom.

Tell her I was here.

Tell her what I said.

Tell her I want

my money back.

Tell her . . ."

CHAPTER 15

nothing is what it seems

I hear the clicking sound first.

Like a toy car shifting gears.

Jimi moves back then foward

then back again.

Kind of in a jerking motion.

The black chair darts out from behind the desk,

moving fast/toward me.

The hum of the motor getting louder.

A high-pitched squeaking sound

stuck in my ears.

Jimi stops on a dime.

Just a foot away.

"I can't run to my mom.

I can't run anywhere."

get up

I'm screaming now.

People are stopping, watching

what's going on.

Security getting close.

"You're faking. Get up."

"I can't. This is how I am.

So if you're going to hit me

give me your best shot." I step

closer and bend down so I'm

at *his* level.

Still not believing what I'm seeing.

"I said, get up." Now I'm in his face.

He's tricking me.

That's what he does.

He lies, and cheats, and steals.

Anything to get what he wants.

Him and his mom.

"That's enough." A security guard

comes between us and grabs my arm,

pulling me back.

"Get off me," I yell, as I feel the guard

tightening his grip.

"It's okay, Ray, this is my brother. It's okay."

"Are you sure?" Ray answers,

not loosening his grip.

"Yeah, it's cool. We're just talkin', that's all."

Ray finally lets me go.

I see V out of the corner of my eye,

motioning wildly for us to leave.

But I'm not going anywhere.

I don't care about that wheelchair.

I still don't believe him.

He's a lie.

He's a thief.

He's *not my brother.*

"let's go somewhere where we can talk"

I stare at Jimi,

shocked and stunned

and still wanting my

revenge.

I look up at the sign next to where it says

INFORMATION/TICKETS,

and see the words: WHEELCHAIR RENTAL.

It's all a scam/just one big scam.

I follow Jimi into the elevator, not saying a word.

Not even looking at him.

Jimi has a shoe box on his lap,

holding it with one hand; with

the other he presses the button that says

Level 3.

The elevator door closes and we start to move.

I should press stop and take care of him now.

We get out where

we came in.

I follow Jimi,

walking behind his chair.

Staring at the wheels spinning on the ground.

I follow him

into the museum café.

A table in the back.

I'm still in attack mode,

but now I'm more confused.

A little unsure of what to do.

Maybe I should push him out of that chair.

Thoughts racing in and out of my mind.

Jimi puts the shoe box on the table.

I just keep staring.

He's still my enemy.

He's still the one who caused us

So much pain.
Who made Mom the way she is,
Who took our life away.
He's still the one.

this is me
"I only use the power chair when I'm at work."
Like I care.
Jimi is talking to me like everything's okay.
Everything is so far from being okay
he's got no idea.
Just because he's in that chair
I still don't care.
"I fell," he says. Like it's no big deal.
"Five years ago, a board was loose in my tree house.
Used to go up there every day.
It was my secret place.
I'm paralyzed, Keith, from the waist down.
It's called an incomplete injury.
My spinal cord is still intact.
Sometimes I can feel something,
maybe a faint sensation,

but that's about it.

I'm not faking,

wish I was. This is the way I am.

This is me."

you owe me

"I don't care.

You still ruined my life.

Even if you are paralyzed, like you say,

it still doesn't take away what you did.

How you stole our money.

Stole our life.

We lost everything.

How is you being in that chair

gonna bring my mom back?

Bring her back from her hell.

Make her well again.

You owe me, Jimi.

More than just money.

Much more than that . . .

And all I want to know is

how you're gonna pay

me back.

Can you tell me?

Huh?

Can you?"

"i miss dad, just like you"

Jimi speaks slow and calm.

But I speak fast and mad:

"He's not your dad.

He was my dad. He was *my* dad

and you stole him from me,

just like you stole everything else."

Jimi is silent. My heart is racing,

I feel my blood pumping.

Jimi puts the shoe box on the table

and taps the lid.

"I'd be mad too.

But there are things you should know.

Things that might help you.

That's why I decided to see you.

I didn't have to, you know.

My mom has no idea about this.

I heard her talking on the phone; she said she got
some e-mail that made her really upset.

I know her password: I saw your e-mail and wrote
you back.

Keith, he was my dad, and that's just a fact.

Just like me and you are brothers."

"Half," I snap back.

"Half," Jimi says, starting a smile, then stopping it
in the middle.

"Half."

letters

Jimi opens the lid to the shoe box.

The brown top faded from time.

He pours tons of letters out onto the table.

Jimi doesn't say a word.

He backs away from the table,

his chair clicking as he moves.

I start reading,

and I can't stop.

Dear Jimi,

Happy seventh B-day. You're gettin' to be a big boy now. Sorry I can't be there to help you blow out your candles. You know I'm full of a lot of hot air. (Ha-ha) But, I'm with you there, in spirit. Have a big piece of cake for me.

Love, always and forever,
Your pops

Dear Jimi,

Hope you liked the guitar I sent. Pretty cool, huh? So happy to hear you're getting into music. Like father like son, right? Miss you lots.

Love, always and forever,
Your pops

Dear Jimi,

Here's a CD of my newest project. I think you're

gonna like it. Kind of retro-rock, but with a
hip-hop feel. How does it feel to hit double digits?
Big Ten. You da man.

Hope to see you soon,
maybe this summer . . .

Love, always and forever,
Your pops

Picking up letters,
picking up the past.

Dear Jimi,

One day you will walk again. You must believe
this like I do. I wish I could take all your pain
away. I will do everything I can to help you.
Everything. Words cannot say how sorry I am.
I should have checked those boards.
Son, I should have checked.
Wish I was there with you right now. I will be
soon. You know I am always by your side

in spirit. Just close your eyes and you'll see me
there I'm right next to you. . . .
Be strong. You will get through this.

Love, always and forever,
Your pops

Dear Denise,

The pain is unbearable knowing I am to blame
for what happened to Jimi. Knowing that I can't
be there nearly as much as I want. As I should.
I am wiring as much money as I can into your
account. You will always have enough money
for whatever you need. Always. I've enclosed this
month's check and payment for the medical bills.
Please let me know if you need anything else.

Be strong.
Love,
MAJ

filling in the blanks

"Dad always liked snail mail.

He said that this way, I would always

have a piece of him. Something I could hold

on to. He was right. He was.

I wasn't allowed to write back.

See, my mom and my dad—our dad—well,

they didn't get along.

Even before my fall.

Mom never had a good thing to say

about him. She blamed him for

her career never going anywhere.

For 'promising her the moon and giving her

a pebble.' I heard that all the time.

I'm glad I kept these, though.

Sure am glad."

Jimi moves closer, but gives me space.

I look up from the letters, hearing Jimi's words.

Jimi filling in the blanks, a little at a time.

Before I know it I'm back

inside the past.

Trying to know more,
trying to know my dad.

Dear Jimi,

I know you are having a hard time with your new life. You're eleven years old, and there are things you want to do, but can't right now.
I know it must be so hard. But things will get better, they will. I promise you.
Jimi, there is something I should have told you before. But I never did.
I think now more than ever you should know.
You have a brother. His name is Keith. He just turned eight. He's a great kid, you'd like him a lot. I call him "Little Cool." 'Cause he's little and he's cool. Get it?
He is truly special, just like you. Loves music, too. And he's good at it just like you! I'll explain more when I see you next. I hope one day the two brothers will meet. One day you two will play ball together. Yes, Jimi, you will play ball again. You will!

Always know that I love you and
am thinking of you every second of
every day.

Be strong.
All my love forever,
Pops

CHAPTER **16**

month after month

my dad wrote to them.

Sending money.

Sending love.

Visiting when he could.

How did he do it?

How did he have the time?

He didn't.

He lied.

To me.

To Mom.

Dad doing the right thing,

but still wrong.

the money

All that money

was for Jimi.

All that money was for him.

From the time he was born,

my dad supported them.

Then, after the accident,

he gave more. He gave

everything he had.

Trying to make things right with money.

Paying all of Jimi's bills,

his hospital stays,

his surgeries.

Dad never gave up hope.

Dad paid for the best rehab,

right here in Cleveland.

Dad paid for

everything.

But it was just too much.

He never had enough cash

to

pay back the savings,

pay back my trust.

To pay back everything he took from us.

So much more than money.

He thought he'd have enough time. . . .

Dear Denise,

Things are tougher here. Biz is very slow. I still
have the money for you and Jimi, don't you

*worry. Had to take from some other places. But
things will pick up and everything will be fine.
It will work out. It always does.
Give my love to Jimi.
He's strong. He's gonna be okay. We're all gonna
be okay.*

*Love,
Maj*

the other child
"I was jealous of you, Keith."
Jimi breaks me out of my trance.
Talking to me again. With that way he has.
I'm catching on—his voice so serious
when he speaks.
Like everything he says, he means.
Everything, so important for me to hear.
"I always felt you were his 'real' son
and I was the 'other child.' You're the
one that got to be with him all the time.
He was there for you on your birthdays.

And after school.

And when you just *needed* him,

he was there.

I didn't have that.

I just saw him every once in a while.

More when I was younger.

As I got older, it was less and less.

Sometimes I feel like it was harder not

having a dad around all these years

than not being able to use my legs.

Sometimes, that's just how I feel."

anger coming back

Trying to make sense of all of this.

The past and the present.

So much to take in.

So much to understand.

It was still wrong.

They were still wrong.

Hearing Jimi, I try to understand what it

was like for him.

I try,

but I can't hold back
my anger.
"Dad *was* there for me, but he
was *always* busy. Time ran out
before we could do all the things we wanted to.
I hear what you're sayin', but you know what?
In the end, *YOU* got the money.
YOU got the name. *YOU* had no right
to all of that. We were left with nothing.
Do you know how hard it's been for me?
For my family?
Do you have any idea?

sitting in silence
Both of us listening
to what the other has to say.
Both of us trying to meet
halfway.
Letting the silence fill up the space.

"they made a mistake,"
Jimi finally says.

"But that mistake made me.

I can't take away what happened.

I can't change the past.

It is what it is, what it was.

I can't give you back what you lost.

We both lost a lot, Keith.

Both of us.

I'll talk to my mom.

Maybe she can help.

Maybe she can give back

some of what she got.

Maybe there's a way,

maybe,

there's a way. . . ."

Jimi smiles.

Reminding me of Dad.

Jimi, trying to help,

trying to heal.

Trying to be

my brother.

hard

I try to let go.

To give Jimi a chance.

Even though I'm not sure—

not sure if I should,

not sure if I can.

This new brother,

accepting me so much.

Accepting who I am.

Seems like it's harder for me.

Harder for me to accept Jimi.

Hard to forget what happened.

His part in all of this.

Hard to forget what Dad did

and what Mom is.

whole again

We meet V back down in the lobby.

She sees that we're okay,

so she lets us go. Giving us time.

Time to get to know each other.

Time to try to become brothers.

I never knew I had a brother,

but Jimi did.

He knew,

but there was nothing he could do.

Couldn't make contact.

'Cause I was with Dad and Mom and—

Jimi knew about all of that.

Dad telling him one day we would meet.

How could we meet?

Dad always so optimistic.

Always thinking everything would work out.

Maybe using that wish, that hope.

Using that to make Jimi believe.

Believe in himself. To stay strong.

To not get down.

To believe he could walk again.

Using me to help Jimi.

A brother waiting for him.

A half brother to help Jimi get whole again.

Jimi's so positive when he talks.

So much at peace with himself/with everyone else.

Jimi and me in the Rock and Roll Hall of Fame.

Seeing our heroes come to life.

Now, seems like we're breaking the ice.

Talking about music and history.

Talking about everything.

Jimi loves Jimi.

Of course.

We spend most of the time back in the

Hendrix exhibit.

Back in the Hendrix theater.

Back in time.

Catching up as we jam with Hendrix,

talking about Dad.

What he was,

what he might have been.

Trying to let go of the hate

and the pain.

Jimi and *me*

trying to get

whole again

and

then that song:

. . . Fly on my sweet angel
Fly on through the sky,
Fly on my sweet angel,
Forever I will be by your side

CHAPTER 11

two weeks
since I met Jimi and I'm tryin'
my best.
Some days it all makes sense.
Some days
it just hurts.
I feel hate towards dad,
but at least I know he tried.
He wasn't a *bad* guy.
He wasn't all good either.
But
he *was* my dad.
I try to keep telling myself that.

Back in school.
Me and V again.
She's my right-hand girl.
I'm her right-hand man.
Walking down the halls
V holds my hand.
Feeling so close to her;
even Bobby Powers can't

take that away.
Bobby Powers
not worth the time of day.
Moved on to a "softer target."
It's Me and V and
now I know Jimi.
Now I know what happened.
The past—the good and bad
and all that in between.
Now I know Jimi.
Now he knows
me.

mom, coming out of her haze
slowly.
Every day, since I've been back.
It seems like she's a *little* better.
Mom softening up/but not too much.
She won't forgive Dad.
But at least she can start to understand.
Know that he *tried* to do the right thing.
"The right thing

isn't going to put food on the table,"

Mom says, still with venom on her tongue.

At least she's starting to sound like Mom again.

Sounding like her fight's comin' back.

I tell her I talked to Jimi today.

He said he was hopeful his

mom would help us out.

We'll see. . . .

A little relief spreads across Mom's face.

A lot on Aunt Berny's.

Mom and Aunt Berny talkin' gossip in the kitchen.

Aunt Berny tellin' me she knew all along she wasn't

talkin' to Mrs. Sweet.

She just let me go. Knew I had to do

what I had to do.

Mom and Aunt Berny

trying to sound like they used to.

Mom, coming out of her haze.

Slowly. . . .

Every day,

seems like

she's a *little* better. . . .

together

My room is dark
almost asleep.
One week goes into two weeks
goes into three.
And tomorrow is the six-month anniversary.
Six months since Dad died.
Six months since the lies died too.
Maybe now I can try to leave the past alone.
Try to keep Dad in my heart—all the good and even
the bad parts.
Get back to my songs
my axe—the *real* love of my life.
Maybe one day me and Jimi *will* play.
We could have a band.
Call it the **Brothers Jam.**
Dig up all Dad's tunes.
We could play the ones I wrote, too.
Put some flames on Jimi's chair,
lights flashin' everywhere.
Keeping my eyes open just long enough, so I can see
the stage.

Dark like my room, but not for long.

So loud I can't hear a thing,

just all the

SCREAMING

FANS.

My eyes closing fast . . .

but not before I see

Dad and

Jimi and

me.

Together for the first time on this stage.

Together for the first time.

Together . . .

ACKNOWLEDGMENTS

I would like to thank the following people who gave me their encouragement, love, moral support, research assistance, great editorial input, and, in one case, a quiet place to write:

Arnold Adoff, Leigh Adoff, Jennifer Besser, Vini Miranda, Susan Graham, Jeff Coplan, Tony James, Garen Thomas, Dorothy Scott, Bill Scott, Michael R. Gray, and Alan M. Warshauer.

Thank you!

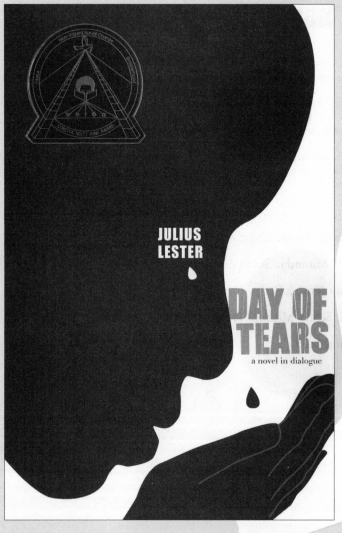